D0539111

# DESERTERS

*by the same author*

AFTER THE RAID

# DESERTERS

CHRIS PALING

JONATHAN CAPE
LONDON

First published 1996

1 3 5 7 9 10 8 6 4 2



First published in the United Kingdom in 1996 by Jonathan Cape,
Random House, 20 Vauxhall Bridge Road, London SW1V 2SA

Random House Australia (Pty) Limited
20 Alfred Street, Milsons Point, Sydney,
New South Wales 2061, Australia

Random House New Zealand Limited
18 Poland Road, Glenfield,
Auckland 10, New Zealand

Random House South Africa (Pty) Limited
PO Box 337, Bergvlei, 2012 South Africa

Random House UK Limited Reg. No. 954009

A CIP catalogue record for this book
is available from the British Library

Papers used by Random House UK Limited are natural,
recyclable products made from wood grown in sustainable forests.
The manufacturing processes conform to the environmental
regulations of the country of origin.

ISBN 0-224-04310-2

Typeset by Deltatype Ltd, Ellesmere Port, Cheshire
Printed and bound in Great Britain by
Mackays of Chatham PLC

*for Julie, whatever*

BEHIND THE BRIGHTON seafront, four or five streets east of the Palace pier, there was a cafe. It was well kept and clean and run by a friend of mine called Barry. It was worth a visit if you could find it, and it wasn't such a bad place to stay either.

I lived there for a while. We were close, Barry and me: the rough and the smooth as his friends used to call us. But everything changed when May turned up. And now the cafe's not there any more. And neither is Barry.

It should never have happened that way. But it did, and I'm sorry.

So this is for you Barry, wherever you are.

# ONE

IT ALL CAME to a head on the day that May was taken into hospital. It was a Monday and Barry was in one of his prissy, tight-lipped moods trying to lay down the law. Sometimes he got so moral he made me want to throw up, especially when you considered some of his sexual tastes. He was very British, Barry, when it came to morality; you could do anything you wanted in the dark but God help you if you ever brought it up the next day. That morning, we'd just had a row over a jacket I'd bought at the Gardner Street market. It was made of two Union Jacks, one of them was upside down so I got it cheap. But Barry knew I didn't have the money to spare so I hid the jacket under the bed until I could find a way of breaking it to him gently.

Finally, on the Monday morning, I just put it on and walked into the living room – trouserless. He tutted a couple of times, then said, 'I refuse to let you out looking like that.'

I said something like, 'Who said anything about going out?'

He looked me up and down then went back to gazing out of the window. He was sitting in the bay in his pink wicker chair with the cat on his knee; backlit by the morning sun, with a faraway look in his eyes. In profile, Barry looked better than front on. He had a goodish patch of fair hair (you couldn't see the bald spot from the side), a slightly beaked nose that was always red from the sun, and blue eyes: sky blue. His eyes were the first thing anybody ever noticed about him. After that, he was something of an anti-climax: middle height, early forties going to fat, stocky legs, a slight stoop from leaning on the counter of the cafe and a rapidly doubling chin. But he photographed well, he always looked good in holiday snaps. In fact he'd have made a creditable Marlene Dietrich the mood he was in that day.

Barry always reckoned he was born to greater things than the cafe, in his head he owned the street. Not that the street was up to much: a few flint cottages built before the town was hijacked by the Prince Regent and his groupies, a pock-marked road, a couple of lock-up garages (IN USE 24 HOURS A DAY. UNDERTAKER. DO NOT OBSTRUCT), and the back-alley door of a pub. The only concession to the fact that we were less than thirty yards from the promenade was the seagull shit on the roofs and the constant racket of traffic on the coast road.

'You look like a lout,' he said, tiring of his view of the street.

In Barry's vocabulary a 'lout' was about as strong a term of abuse as he could throw at you. A 'lout' to Barry was a member of the working class, with all the brutal, uncivilised connotations that held for him. His father was big in the Gas Board and Barry, like most first-generation refugees from his class, denied his roots with a passion that the middle classes could only guess at. And when he used the word, he sent it into the world with a slight cluck so that it came out as 'lart' (I don't know if you've heard that toffee-nosed art critic, but that's how Barry sounded when he used the word). I'd cultivated a loutish image to survive my spell in the army, but it was no worse than Barry's pretensions. It just meant that whenever we went out together, I took every opportunity to confirm his worst prejudices.

I don't want to give the impression I didn't like Barry. I did. And sometimes it even went beyond that. There were times when I'd watch him behind the counter of the cafe or when he was asleep and feel just everything for him. But towards the end it didn't happen often, and never when he was trying to wind me up by using my proper name.

'You never cease to amaze me, Clifford.' (This, of course, was him again.)

I bit back. 'Don't call me Clifford.'

'Why not?'

'It rankles me. Call me Dave.'

'Dave? It was Frank yesterday.'

'Was it? I've never been consistent. You know that. I've paid a high price for it too. A bird once accused me of being sexually schizophrenic. There's a name for it: something Latin.'

That stopped him for a second. If he'd really been in the mood for a row it was at that point he'd have started in on my perverse past – a past which embraced rampant heterosexuality. That was something he never forgave me for. I don't think Barry hated women, he just couldn't fathom them and didn't understand how anybody could find anything remotely attractive in them. I suppose, given a lengthy period under a shrink, the roots of this would have emerged in the relationship he had with his mother.

She, apparently, hated her own father and spent her entire married life (in a poor London terrace two tube stops from suburbia, with two sons and no daughter, desperation held partly at bay by the sweet sherry taken three times a day before meals) taking it out on Barry's father. Barry felt a huge compassion for his dad – but his dad devoted all of his energies trying to make his wife feel something for him. Barry (and his elder brother) were squeezed out by them both. He claimed that the first inkling he had about his sexuality came when he was at junior school and caught sight of a boy undressing. He confided this peculiar longing to his mother who, rather than attempting to understand it, beat the living daylights out of him then took him to their GP for a good talking to. And there the story may have ended except for the fact that their GP was an undeclared pederast and initiated Barry into the very practices he was supposed to be warning him off. As a result, Barry's sexuality was frozen at the age of initiation and his quest for sexual satisfaction never entirely free from fantasies of domination by figures of authority. There was a period in his adolescence when he was never away from the doctor's surgery, his sad parading of fictitious minor ailments scant camouflage for his desire to be given a good seeing to by his new GP.

Barry finally broke cover in his early twenties and it's no coincidence that his second coming (with a taxi driver, in a public toilet at the top of a small municipal park) occurred on the journey back home from his mother's funeral. His father is still alive but I've never met him. Apparently he now lives in Eastbourne with a woman who used to work in his Gas showroom. His name is Bert, hers is Dora, and that's all I feel I want to know about them. Anyway, Barry had a deep suspicion of anybody who crossed the line, and my period of heterosexuality troubled him deeply, which is why I tormented him with it so much, and why he could never let my torments pass unchallenged.

'You're completely unaware of the effect you have on others, aren't you,' he said, fixing those blue eyes on me in a way that made me feel he could almost see through me. 'You could be taken for a hardened criminal. You frighten me sometimes.'

'Do I? I don't mean to.' Though of course I did. It wasn't just the fact that he was in poor shape and I took a pride in looking after myself, it was also something else to do with his pretence. He liked to pretend we were just a happily married couple. Deep down he knew it was all bollocks, but Barry rarely got deep down. His life was lived like a stylus clogged with dust, never properly making contact with the record it was supposed to be reproducing.

Barry was frightened by my lack of inhibitions yet at the same time I think that that's what attracted him to me. But we were bickering, nothing serious, just sparring together to pass the time. It must have been about mid-morning, after the early rush, we'd gone upstairs to put our feet up. The cafe was pretty quiet except for the regulars: the woman from the flower shop, in for her cuppa and sandwich after wiring up the wreaths and bouquets for the day, a couple of traders from the grocer's stall moaning about the quality of produce at New Covent Garden, and a dosser, sheltering from the breeze until we had to kick him out because the stink was putting off anybody else from coming in.

We employed an old girl to help us out in the cafe after the breakfast rush. But every so often she'd get a crowd in and call one of us downstairs. Cafe life: boredom interspersed with periods of frantic activity – frantic but still boring. She shouted out, 'Custom!' and I offered to go down.

'No. I don't want you frightening my clientele away.' (That was typical Barry for you – 'clientele', never just trade.)

'That's why I got this blazer,' I tried. 'It's made of two Union Jacks. One's upside down. That's how it found its way to the market.'

'Put some trousers on. It might soften the effect.' Barry was being masterful and I never liked to deflate him in those moments, so I just swallowed it and said, 'I'll come down when I've changed, shall I?'

'If you must. And wake her up. She can do the laundry for a change.'

The *her* of course, was May. Barry couldn't often bring himself to mention her by name, they never entirely saw eye to eye, but he couldn't get her out of her room. He felt a peculiar sort of compassion for her, like you might have for a tarred, broken seagull on the beach; a compassion tinged with the feeling that part of the responsibility was his.

But May wasn't in. I'd heard the door go before five. She was sleeping badly: an early warning. Madness was coming through the night for her again, knocking on the door as she slept, prodding her awake, giving her the night sweats and the dreams of lost children. Poor May, she rarely cried out loud but inside she was usually in tears.

I told Barry she'd gone out. He snapped, 'Tell her when she comes back then.'

'I might,' I said (there was only so much of this masterful stuff you could take).

'Just do it, will you.'

'Was that a threat?'

'No.' He blanched, beginning to crumble.

'Sounded uncannily like it to me.'

'It wasn't intended . . . Oh, I don't know. I don't know.' He breathed out a long sigh. The cafe bell sounded. Another punter had wandered off into the petrol fumes of the morning without waiting for his cuppa.

'You can't afford to turn away custom like that. Not with your precarious financial plight,' I said, trying to drag him back from the edge of a day teetering towards serious misery.

His eyes flicked back to life. 'You take a real delight in destruction, don't you?'

'It passes the time. Anyway, I might not stay here much longer. You might get off relatively unscathed.' This was another line of torment I employed. The truth of it was that I'd been thinking of moving on for some time; it was only the comfort of the cafe that kept me there. I didn't feel any loyalty to Barry and I think he knew that. Actually, I've never felt any loyalty to anybody. I sometimes wonder if I haven't got a defective gene or something.

But the threat of me leaving had again sown the seeds of insecurity in Barry's tortured mind, enough for him to chuck the cat on the floor and leap up, hands in his pockets, staring at me like a nutter.

'What do you mean you might not stay here!'

'Yes, I've been giving some thought to moving on – and the more I think about it the more the idea appeals.'

'But I thought . . . ' he said, and then stopped half way through his plea like only people in films seem to do, though it was a ploy Barry employed regularly.

'Go on,' I prompted.

'I thought you . . . we, you know, you and me, had an arrangement.'

'Do we? I don't remember signing anything when you first brought me back here.'

That was a sordid night if ever there was one. I'd fetched up in Brighton after hitching along the coast from Dover. It was late so I decided to pitch tents for the night and wandered round the town looking for some cheap action or someone drunk enough to take a few quid off. I found Barry in a small Victorian bar close to the pier. The pub was bloody horrible inside: red flock wallpaper, the walls covered with pictures of drag acts. The place was thick with smoke, pairs of pale faces peered out from each dark alcove. If it hadn't been last orders I'd have gone somewhere else. Barry was trying to pick up a youngish lad who was laughing in his face; he was pissed out of his mind which made him a perfect mark. I got rid of the youth and Barry offered me a drink, when he paid I took a good look inside his wallet.

I knew from his eagerness that Barry was interested. He was desperate, but in a kind of endearing way which made his desperation attractive. Then I suppose came the moment when it all happened. I saw something in him that made nicking his wallet seem more disgusting than it actually was. To come clean about it, in fact I caught a glimpse of myself leaning towards him in the bar mirror. It was so ludicrous and so disconnected an image I almost shouted to him to watch his pockets because someone was trying to pick them. When I saw it was me I stopped and stared at myself; maybe it was the first time I'd taken a close look for a few days. I saw someone who was no longer a boy. Someone who had good enough looks once but had all but destroyed them with booze and the needle. I saw a black leather jacket hanging on a wasted frame. Black hair fighting free of an army crew-cut and hard, wary eyes staring out like a fox from a bush. I'd always had good bones – women always envied me my cheeks – but the flesh between them was white and taut. I realised I'd hardly eaten anything for over a week. I was making the most of my freedom from army regulations and any hunger I did feel had been stifled by nicotine and alcohol. I looked like a Dickensian sneak thief and for all my faults I've never been entirely comfortable with petty theft.

Anyway, I told myself to stop and I stopped. And when I did I remembered that I hadn't got anywhere to stay for the night so I decided to let him take me home and then maybe just liberate a few pounds from him the following morning to help me on my way.

At just past eleven we rolled back to the cafe, Barry leading, explaining in rolling drunken logic how owning a cafe wasn't his ideal way of making a living and that he didn't intend to do it for much longer. But I liked the place as soon as I saw it. It was wrapped round the corner of a Victorian street full of grocers and fishmongers and other small-scale traders, and a street full of older cottages. The sea was at the bottom, less than a hundred yards away.

The cafe took up the ground floor of a three-floor building. Barry had painted the outside walls round the tall windows green. It felt continental and bohemian, an atmosphere that survived despite the cheap scuffed tables inside. He had a knack for design which transformed the humdrum into the extraordinary with just a lick of paint here and a bit of material there. I told him I liked it and he was pleased. Then I helped myself to a fry up while Barry went upstairs to do something to himself. When he came down I didn't hear him and he must have stood for a few minutes watching me eat. I was sitting at one of the tables surrounded by sauce bottles. Barry had put on some cheap scent and a cravat. I nearly choked when I saw that, he looked like the Duke of Windsor on his hols. He stormed off when I laughed and I heard a door slam upstairs so I took my time finishing off and then I washed up and cleaned round the kitchen a bit before shutting off the lights and finding my way to his bedroom.

I tried a few doors before I found his then I walked in without knocking. A small bedside light gave the room a warm orange glow. He was lying in bed, staring piously at the ceiling like a crusader on a tomb. Looking at him I felt as though we'd known each other a long time, much longer than the two hours it actually was. It seemed right just being there, I knew he felt the same, as though the row was one in a series and we knew it had run its course and now the time had come to enjoy the making up. I climbed into bed after kicking off my boots, then I thought I'd better go and wash and tried to get out. But Barry just pulled me towards him and kissed me full on the lips. I woke alone nine hours later feeling as though somehow I'd come home. Anyway, it was too late to carry out the previous night's plan of nipping off with his cash before he woke up.

I walked naked to the window and threw the curtains open. An old lady tugging a shopping trolley behind her saw me and waved as if she knew me. I waved back. The sun was new and perfect; it was body temperature, like velvet. The air had an edge to it so you could feel it going into your nostrils and down into your chest and I felt happy. (This might not seem like much to you but I can only remember a couple of times in my life when I've actually experienced what I now recognise as real happiness. Those moments usually come when I'm alone. They're always at the beginning of something new. And the sun is always shining. Sad but true.) The dread I'd been carrying seemed to have gone. Once again, like the night before, I felt like I was on familiar ground.

I was ashamed to put on what I'd been wearing last night so I borrowed some of Barry's clothes. He was stockier than me but we were about the same height. I put on a pair of his black denims tied up with a belt and topped it off with a black turtleneck sweater. His wardrobe was perfect; all the clothes were squared off and ironed like new. I went downstairs and sat at one of the tables and eventually he brought over my breakfast. We didn't say anything and that mattered somehow. His clothes were mine for the taking, his food was mine, what he was getting from me was something only he'd know. But that's how it began, about two years before. Perhaps he was remembering all that as I tormented him about moving on.

'As far as I understood it I was to be free to come and go as I pleased.'

'And so you are,' he said, a bit too eagerly.

'Fine. That's alright then isn't it.'

'But not for good.' He threw in the plea with a cock of his head.

'Oh Barry. Would I leave you? Could I leave you? You're the nearest thing to a mother I ever had.'

'Oh fuck off!' He rarely swore, but he hated it when I took the rise out of him while we were arguing.

'Only I never met a mother who didn't pine for her brood till the day she died. It's a thankless task bar a few years at the outset when the little creatures trick you into thinking you're the most important things in their lives. My mother wasn't fooled, I can tell you. She saw it for what it was at the outset.' Sometimes I told him more when he thought I was taking the mickey than I ever did when he believed I was being serious.

'She's been talking to you has she?'

'My mother? No, as you well know, we haven't been in touch for some years.'

He brushed me off impatiently. 'No *her*, May, she put you up to this, didn't she? I bet it was her that loaned you the money for that ridiculous blazer.'

It was, as a matter of fact, I didn't deny it. But it felt uncomfortable as an admission even though I couldn't really pinpoint who it was I was betraying: him or her. I never felt I could do justice to both of them and I still don't know whether that was more to do with them or me. May often loaned me money; sometimes she bought me things, but more often she'd nick them for me from the shops. I used to window-shop along Western Road then go back and tell her what I wanted. Then she'd go and stuff whatever I'd picked out under her dress. Sometimes we went together, sometimes she was seen, but they rarely caught her – or me. We were both good runners, and after we'd legged it we'd end up in some back alley laughing like idiots. But May was another trigger of Barry's paranoia.

'She wants you to leave with her, doesn't she?' He was still strutting round the room, burning off his anxiety, with his hands locked tight in his pockets.

I had to let him off. 'No, what sort of a future could she offer me? She couldn't keep me in the manner to which I've become accustomed.'

'So I'm just a meal ticket to you. Is that it?' he said pitifully.

'Don't underestimate yourself, Barry. Your heart's in the right place.' He didn't know how to take that, but I was getting bored with the conversation. Once Barry was in his self pity groove it repeated until you nudged him on with a bigger problem.

'I think I might go out,' I said. 'Take a walk along the prom.'

The phone started ringing. Barry lunged for it. He loved the phone, he'd talk on it all day given the opportunity. As he lifted the receiver he said, 'When will you be back?'

'I don't know.'

'Wait, will you.'

'See you Barry.' I started walking out.

'Wait!'

I would have gone but it was immediately apparent that the call was about May. It seemed she'd been nicked again and then flipped like she had a tendency to do. She ended up periodically in the nut house where they'd fill her full of drugs that brought her down with a bang and made her mouth dry and really screwed up the mechanisms in her head. Then they'd let her out again and she'd be alright for a few months.

'She's back on the ward.' Barry put down the phone. 'Go and see her will you. She listens to you . . . and take her some flowers from me.' When it came to the crunch, Barry's compassion always won out.

'No. We're not speaking.' We'd had a bust up the night before. It was never all roses with May. A few months earlier she'd taken it upon herself to try and trace my mother in the misguided belief that I actually wanted to meet the woman. I didn't. I've never had much desire to meet either her or my father. I've no stomach for sentiment. I told all this to May but it didn't register. May has a sentimental streak in her that's fine when she's in control but when she's not it becomes very wearing. She buys toys for her room and looks longingly at babies in prams, all that sort of thing. The roots of her madness lay that way. I knew she'd lost a child somewhere down the line.

I filled Barry in with the details, but something had triggered his paranoia again. 'She's dangerous,' he said. 'She wants to take you away.'

'What could I do?'

'What did you do?'

'I did what any self-respecting man would in that situation: I hit her.' I hate hitting women. It's a sign that they've managed to goad you further than you wanted to go. Women can get much deeper into you than men. With men it's a completely different ballgame; you can hit out in blind anger or just for the fun of it.

'After you'd hit her,' he pressed, 'what then?'

'Nothing. She's not my responsibility.'

'She's not anybody's responsibility. That's her problem. Go and see her, I can't leave the cafe.'

'Yeah. I might.'

Barry flipped again at that and went puce. 'Why don't you do something useful for a change!' He stamped his foot, the floor rocked, the sash windows rattled, the old girl called 'Oy!' from the cafe downstairs.

'What? And break the habit of a lifetime? I've got my reputation to preserve you know.'

'Just do it will you!' He was almost choking on his anger. He had no more stops to pull out.

'I might. But for her, not for you.'

I walked out. By then, things were so wrong between us that we were enjoying the rows much more than the moments of calm. I could sense it was time for moving on. As it happened, it came sooner rather than later, and not in a way I'd have chosen for either of us.

# TWO

I WALKED OUT through the cafe ignoring a couple of the regulars who looked up, anticipating some banter. An old man was fighting to get through the door but somehow he'd got his Sainsbury's bag caught round the handle. I pushed past him harder than I should; he looked hurt, then angry. I swore at him and straightaway wished I hadn't. I hated not being in control. It was always other people that tipped me off balance, and when that happens there's nothing for it but to leave.

I walked down to the Steine and stood around by the Pavilion waiting for a bus. The sun was making a tame attempt to show its face from behind the clouds. I perched on the railings watching the traffic. I half decided to go there and then but it didn't feel finished; you leave a part of yourself behind when there are loose ends still to be tied, or at least you're always looking over your shoulder for the past to creep up on you.

The bus finally came, dispersing the mood that was threatening to make me throw myself beneath it. I took a seat upstairs and it jolted off, forcing itself into the traffic and drawing the cat-calls of car horns as it did so. The town went by at street level. Occasionally we'd stop for a short queue of unsmiling citizens who'd shuffle on and wave all manner of passes at the driver claiming insanity, disability or blindness. Nobody seems to pay for public transport any more; if I contributed taxes the situation would piss me off no end.

The bus wheezed up the steep hill towards the racecourse then disgorged its cargo of hospital visitors. I followed the procession of bent denizens through the gates and into the body of the hospital.

If you haven't been there I should describe the hospital to you. The walls of the place are stained black with grime; if it wasn't built as a Victorian lunatic asylum then it looks as if it should have been. It hugs the top of a hill at the edge of the town, a tall chimney protrudes above the wall that surrounds it and the setting is not improved by the severe lack of greenery. It's the most cheerless place I've ever been, there are sights in that hospital which would make you cry. And May was in there again.

With a few rudimentary questions I found the ward she was on. When I walked in the first thing I saw was an old woman rocking back and forth, her legs hanging loose from a high bed. She was dressed, coat buttoned tight, with her small suitcase on the floor, but it was clear she wasn't going anywhere. Some of the beds had sprawled figures in them, like drunks after an all-night party. There was a stench of urine and an air of expectancy about the place. But not a pleasant air. Not the exciting air of anticipation you feel when you're waiting for a singer to sing, more of the impending doom of an awaited hanging. But May wasn't on the ward, or even in the smoke-filled television room with its scattered incomplete jigsaws, tense teary conversations and manic monologues from the repertory company of wild-eyed inmates. That meant only one thing: they'd put her in the cell for her own protection.

The cell was at the end of a long corridor, out of earshot of the main ward. I peered through the small window in the thick door. May was curled up in the far corner hugging her knees to her chest. I tapped on the glass. She looked left and right, unable to trace where the noise had come from. I knocked again, this time with the edge of a coin, and now she saw me. At first she didn't seem to recognise me. Then it registered and she mouthed something through the window. I motioned for her to come closer so I could hear her. She dragged herself over like a dog that had been hit by a car.

'It took you long enough,' she shouted, then pushed at the door. 'See? They've locked me in.'

'I'm here now May . . . are you alright?' Words let you down at moments like that.

She shouted something about her clothes and started pawing at her nightdress, taking fistfuls of the fabric then letting it fall. It was several sizes too big for her and a washed-out pink, or perhaps she just had it on inside out.

'What brought this on May?'

'Too many things,' she said sharply. 'I had a list as long as my arm: shopping and . . . ' She waved in a wide gesture that encompassed the rest of the list. I imagine it included the laundry, the cleaning, the washing up, the shopping. All the chores we were supposed to share but which she inevitably avoided. ' . . . I don't know,' she went on, vaguely, 'all the usual things.' Concern flicked over the face again like a cloud crossing the sun. She said, 'I hate brown envelopes, don't you?' Then she went through a long, paranoid spiel about envelopes and officialdom.

It was a shock to see May like that; the fluency of her movements made leaden by the medication. The real May has a ballet dancer's fragile grace and a quiet wide-eyed beauty that looks as if it may be in its last flowering. She has long fair hair and a waif-like face. Her beauty is something that looks as though it needs protecting – an endangered species. But even that is not what it seems. I once saw a butterfly whose outstretched wings looked like the face of an owl: beautiful and fake and . . . fragile; a word you would always associate with May.

'What happened?' I shouted. May shook her head with disbelief – whether this was in response to the question or her circumstances I was unsure – then she went back to the corner of the cell, slumped to the floor and began a conversation with herself. She posed questions then answered them with a shake of her head. Occasionally she seemed to be looking for elucidation; once or twice she shivered.

It was clear I couldn't leave her there for much longer. May was held together with thread. Sometimes it came a little loose, but I'd never seen it break altogether. Any longer in there and I knew she'd come apart at the seams. I waved and mouthed that I'd be back; she pretended not to have noticed. I held my fingertips to the glass and they drew her like a magnet; she came tentatively back to the door and pressed her cheek against the small window. I could see she was starting to break so I blew her a kiss and left. I made up my mind to spring her that evening. I knew that if I went through the formal channels they wouldn't let her out until they were ready, and by then it would be too late.

I walked back down the hill, savouring the freedom and wondering what I was letting us both in for. I knew that if I succeeded in getting May out of the hospital we wouldn't be able to stay in the town. It was then I realised I'd provided myself with the excuse I'd been looking for to leave Barry and the cafe for good. Thinking about the cafe took me back to the year before when May had arrived, having been drawn in by the 'Room to Let' sign in the window. It must have been winter because Barry rented the rooms on a weekly basis during the season. I was minding the cafe alone while Barry got something done to his feet; he always had problems with bunions. May trooped in with her carpet bag, bought a cup of tea and went to sit by the window. She didn't really register with me at first: as far as I could tell she was just another drifter on her way through the town. Then I caught her staring at me as she drank her tea. She had a kind of silent movie sadness about her: wide, expressive eyes peering from a chalk-white face. She seemed to be sizing me and the cafe up, as though she'd been brought in to decorate and she was trying to work out how much paper she was going to need. Finally she carried her empty cup back to the counter and asked me about the room to let. I said something about her having to talk to Barry about it, but she was insistent that I let her have it there and then. She said the place was just right for her, and she'd known it the moment she'd walked in. She wanted it so much that I soon gave in and helped her carry her bag upstairs.

While she unpacked I sat on the bed and watched her. Looking back it seems like something you just wouldn't do with somebody you've only just met, but she was one of those people you feel you know without having to go through the usual rituals. We didn't talk much, I just sat there while she pulled out her dolls, and her clothes, and a square of silk that she threw over the small table before putting her silver model of the Eiffel Tower on it, then the Tower of London calendar. After that, her alarm clock came out, three or four 7″ records, a pile of long thin dresses, a hairbrush with its handle tied up with silk scarves, a bundle of underwear that she sneaked into a drawer so that I couldn't see, and a framed photograph of a baby which she unwrapped carefully from tissue paper before setting it squarely in the centre of the table. She brushed her hands then sat next to me on the bed as if to say that she was now settled.

I was glad I'd let her have the room but when Barry hobbled back from the chiropodist he went mad. I couldn't face a row so I went out for a drink and left him to sort it out. When I got back I expected to find her gone, but she was downstairs in the cafe and Barry was behind the counter looking sullen and depressed. May was sitting on a table, her feet up on a chair, and holding court to the regulars about how she'd just been beaten up by her husband and needed somewhere to stay. It was all lies of course, but Barry knew that if he threw her out after that performance he'd lose half of his customers too.

Later that night, when I was alone with Barry, I asked him why he'd got so cross about me letting her the room. He wouldn't say for a while, but when I pressed him he burst into tears, which was not like him at all. It seems he'd had a dream in which a woman arrived and took me away with her. But what he couldn't figure was the fact that the day May arrived the 'Room to Let' sign hadn't been in the window. He never found out how she got to know about his room. Of course, considering what happened later, his premonition was spot on, but at the time I invested a good deal of effort in reassuring him that there couldn't possibly be anything between me and his new lodger.

Sometimes I wonder what did draw us together. I saw someone on the telly once who said we look to others for what we can't find in ourselves. In that sense May was like a negative of me, but how then did Barry fit in? I suppose all three of us overlapped like the Olympic circles. Barry and May and me, sewn together, made quite a respectable whole – though it was Barry, of course, who contributed the respectability. He knew what I felt for May, which is why he was frightened of her. I suppose if Barry and May had managed to work things out between them, then we'd have all lived happily ever after. But they couldn't, so we didn't.

When I reached the bottom of the hospital hill, I crossed the patch of scrub grass and dog shit that passed for a park before heading into one of the older areas of the town. The North Laines had been tarted up in the seventies. For nearly a century it was the slum area of town with its narrow streets and crowded, damp cottages. The council were going to flatten it in the sixties but some sandal-wearers got up a petition and saved it. Now the windows are plastered with Greenpeace stickers, the residents are up in arms about parking problems and everybody pretends they're living in Chelsea. Still it remains a choice area for decent pubs.

I walked into the Eastern but didn't spot anybody I knew. I didn't have many friends of my own – most were mutual acquaintances I'd got to know through Barry – but I fancied some company.

I slammed down a couple of pints then went out to the Gents to roll a joint. Someone followed me in, but I didn't feel the need so I told him in no uncertain terms where to go. He started badmouthing me, he was only a kid really, so I smacked him round a couple of times and he scampered off back into the pub. The marijuana lifted me high enough to lose the stench of the Gents from my nostrils and I walked on air back into the bar and ate a couple of bags of pork scratchings which I washed down with two or three more pints. I fell into conversation with an old bloke in a raincoat at the bar. He told me he used to work on the local rag, but after a while everything he said began to sound familiar, as though he'd said it before, and I felt like I wasn't making much sense either. We could have stayed that way all afternoon, talking garbage to each other, getting more and more drunk, but through the misted windows I could see it was threatening rain so I left the raincoat to his fags and beer. He said goodbye to me by name. It seemed strange. The day was getting stranger as it went on.

The sky was purple when I walked out onto the street, the air cold and heavy. I saw the youth who had approached me in the Gents standing in the doorway of the shop opposite. His pose (hands deep in pockets, casually leaning against the wall) suggested that he was trying to look like a model from a jeans advert, but he succeeded only in looking like a low-grade rent boy. He tried to sneer but it came out as a half smile; his bottom lip was cut which provoked a momentary sense of guilt and a huge amount of sadness but it soon passed.

I jogged back to the cafe and just made it before the skies opened. I couldn't get May out of my mind. The envelope she'd been ranting about kept coming back, nagging to be acknowledged. I feared it might have something to do with the enquiries she'd been making about my mother, but I was too drowsy from the drink even to consider the implications. I decided to get my head down for a couple of hours before going back to the hospital to spring her. Barry collared me on the way upstairs.

'How is she?' he said, meaning how was I.

'May? Yes. Fine . . . well, no, not fine, but she'll live.'

I hung onto the banisters, but I didn't want to go up. I knew that this could be our last conversation and I wanted to remember it. I also wanted to fix Barry in my mind: behind the counter of his little cafe in his apron, tea towel over his arm, urn steaming behind him, slight smile of satisfaction teasing his face. For all his protests about cafe life not being for him I can't think of anyone better suited to it. He made people feel good about coming in, he had a generous nature; a rare humanity. He could see through me, but most of the time we rubbed along together it was necessary for us to pretend that he couldn't. It would have made our life together too painful and too complicated if we'd both acknowledged that sooner or later I was destined to leave. But as I waited on the stairs I think we both realised at the same time that the end was in sight.

'What did she have to say?' he said, trying to force the focus away from the inevitable.

'Sent her love and said don't you dare rent her room out.' I offered him a smile, but he looked away and started wiping the counter with a cloth.

'That sounds . . . sounds as if she's on the mend then.'

'Yeah.' I waited, offering him a chance to say what was really on his mind. But he continued wiping, sighing heavily, his mouth was creased into concern. A kid came up to the counter asking for a teaspoon for his mother, Barry managed a quick smile as he produced one with a flourish from a drawer. He gave the child a Mars bar, the boy looked at it waiting for the catch. The cafe was close to a block of flats where some of the kids lived lives in which nothing was offered unconditionally. Barry kept his eye out for those children; he had a talent for making them feel good about themselves. Maybe that's why I stayed with him for as long as I did.

I couldn't stand it any longer. I told Barry I was going up and took the stairs two at a time. I lay on the sofa trying to sleep but the anxiety and the traffic kept me awake. I stalked around for a while wondering whether or not to go and talk it out with him. But when I finally did go down Barry used it as an excuse to go upstairs and put his feet up. He hadn't grasped the urgency of the situation; having spent two years together I don't imagine he expected me to leave at such short notice.

As I stood behind the counter, an old man shuffled up proffering an empty cup like a beggar. 'You going to apologise?' he snarled. It was the man I'd sworn at when I'd stormed out earlier on. He was short – about five foot five, and he was thin under his grey mac. He was wearing a brown felt hat with a bus pass tucked under the hatband. His hands were knobbly with arthritis and his long face was of an uncertain shape, the skin draped over old bones like a coat thrown over the back of a chair. I'm sure, like a bloodhound, he would have looked completely different lying down. But there was still fight in his eyes which peered out, magnified to twice their size by the thick lenses of his specs.

'Yeah,' I said, 'I'm sorry.'

'You don't look sorry.'

'What do you want – a signed apology?'

'It's Cliff, isn't it?'

'Yeah. Sometimes,' I said grudgingly.

'Queer are you – like him?' He gestured upstairs.

'Yeah. Sometimes.'

'Can't understand it myself.' He paused for reflection before offering me the next instalment of his opinions. 'I can't ever see myself fancying a bloke.'

'Course you can. You just don't admit it.'

'No I can't. Honest.' He peered worriedly through his glasses to judge whether I'd misunderstood what he was trying to say to me.

'It's fascination is it then, that brings you in here? Come to see the animals in the zoo?'

'It passes the time.' He looked round at the sorry collection of humanity we'd trawled in the cafe that afternoon. It was like a study in still life in there. Besides a couple of the regulars, one of them asleep over a paper, there was a woman from the flats with a toddler who was toying with the salt cellar. The woman looked completely out of it; as though she either didn't care or didn't want to care, but the kid was well dressed and didn't show any visible sign of bruising like some that used the cafe. 'I like it in here,' the old bloke went on. 'Your mate's not bad. He's got a heart of gold. Not like you.'

'Me?' I was taken aback by his frankness.

'You'll come to a sticky end you will boy.' He waved an arthritic finger at me, the knuckles like the end of a briar walking stick. 'You can't go throwing your weight around like you do without running into trouble one day.'

'I'm a good runner.'

'You'd bloody better be.'

'Another tea is it?' I lifted the heavy pot and threatened his empty cup with it.

'Naah.' He waved me away.

'Go on. Have it on the house.'

'Alright.' He pushed his cup and saucer forwards as if it was he who was doing me the favour. I topped him up and he took out his cigarettes and tamped one on the box. They were untipped Capstans. 'Do you want one?' He caught me staring at the ochre box.

'Thanks.'

He lit up and blew out the first lungful of smoke before picking a sliver of tobacco from his lip. His fingers were burnt conker brown by a lifetime of serious nicotine addiction.

'I only started coming in here when the missus went,' he said, chewing his thumbnail. The nicotine rush had transported him back in time.

'Left you did she,' I joshed, 'for another bloke?'

'Cancer.' He breathed out the word with solemnity and respect. 'Cancer' like 'heart attack' and, to a lesser extent, 'arthritis' carried a weighty baggage of associations. In each of those words is enough material to keep an average pensioner in anecdotes for the best part of an evening.

I decided to deny him the opportunity of giving me the unexpurgated version. 'I'm not bloody surprised if she smoked those things,' I said with what I hoped was enough lightness to mask the callousness of the observation.

'No, she was on tipped.'

'Just goes to show then doesn't it.'

'You need places to go when you get left like that.' He gave me a pleading look. 'We never needed anyone when we were together.'

'. . . No?' I gave the comment the space it deserved, sensing that perhaps I was hearing something that nobody had listened to before.

'I never thought I really needed her.' He laughed bitterly. 'We limped along, you know, like you do.'

'No, I don't know,' I said honestly. 'It's not something I recognise.'

'She never smiled much . . . I used to see younger women. If they smiled I thought they were everything.' He peered deeper into the smog of his past. 'You know, I even had a couple of flings . . . She never knew. I was always back before the night was out . . . she never knew.'

'Why are you telling me this?'

'Because you haven't heard it yet.'

'What makes you think I'm interested?'

'You're probably not. I don't care. I'm a lonely old man. You're supposed to humour lonely old men.'

I'd tricked him out of his reminiscing. His past was too valuable to be entrusted to someone who couldn't see the value in it. 'I hope somebody puts me out of my misery before I get like you,' I said.

'They will, boy. They will.'

'But why did you stay with her? If you were so bloody miserable?'

'It was easier than leaving.'

'That's fine indictment of the marital state.'

'You could put it on the gravestones of most people I know.'

'How depressing.'

'That's why you stay with him upstairs isn't it?' He leant a little towards me over the counter.

'Not really. It's more than that.'

'You're going, aren't you?' he said through a crafty smile.

'Why do you say that?'

'I recognise the look. You don't care any more, do you?'

'If I was, you wouldn't be the first to know.'

'Don't count on it, boy. Your friend's got no idea. None at all. I see it. I see it all from that table over there.'

I could have told him different, but I didn't. 'Yeah, well, you won't tell him, will you, grandad?'

'Me! Nobody listens to a word I say. Cheerio.' He drained his cup, picked up his cigarettes and began to walk out. 'You will suffer boy,' he called back, 'I can see that. You're going to get hurt.'

He lunged at a plate on a table by the door and sent it smashing against the wall, then he laughed and walked out. Nobody seemed to register what he'd done. The child looked up briefly then went back to playing with the salt. I decided to let Barry clear up the mess so I called him down and walked out when I heard him on the stairs.

# THREE

I WALKED DOWN the street and stared at the pier for a few minutes. No matter how many times you see it, the pier always comes up fresh and surprising; like a greenhouse on a jetty teasing the waves beneath it to reach up and smash it to pieces. I was always invigorated by the audacity of it. When I got back, the cafe was empty except for the regular still asleep over his *Racing Post*. I walked up behind him and coughed as loudly as I could into his ear. He nearly jumped through the roof.

'Why did you do that!' he squealed, rubbing his ear.

'You were asleep.'

'So?'

'This is a cafe not a hotel. Sod off elsewhere if you want a kip.' His name was Fat Will. He was a ponce.

'That's nice that is. Bloody marvellous.'

I bent down close to his face so that Barry couldn't hear. 'I said fuck off, we're closing.'

He lurched out of his chair, full of pomposity. 'You won't catch me in here again,' he said, then reeled towards the door, blinking away the sleep.

'Hear that, Barry?' I called. 'Fat Will's not coming in here again.'

'Leave him alone.' Barry was looking at Fat Will as if to apologise for my behaviour.

'Why should I?'

'Just leave it. Cheerio, Will.' Barry threw him a healing smile and the ponce stormed out. The bell rang as the door clicked shut. 'You're in a nice mood today, aren't you?' Barry was wiping the counter down again as he opened the hostilities.

'He gets on my tits, that's all. You let people like him walk all over you.'

'I think that's my business isn't it?'

'Some business, Barry.' I pushed past him and went upstairs. He didn't follow me up, I could hear him shutting up shop, throwing the bolt on the door, turning round the 'Sorry we're closed – even for Old Holborn' sign, collecting the few cups left on the tables. I sat for a while on the top step listening to him, knowing how much I was going to miss the domestic predictabilities of the cafe.

It was late afternoon and time to go. I really had nothing to lose by then. At least that's what I thought. In truth I had everything to lose and I lost it through May. Looking back now, I suppose it was because I thought I could save her, and in saving her I thought she might repay the compliment. And I was also in love with her in an odd way. One afternoon we were messing around in her bedroom and suddenly we were on her bed and she was kissing me and I was kissing her. The next thing we were struggling out of our clothes, and locked together tight, but enjoying every minute of it. Afterwards we lay together like kids on a beach. It wasn't something we repeated, but we both got a simple pleasure out of it.

I went back to plotting our escape. The priority was to get hold of some cash, I knew Barry wasn't going to stump up a going away present without a certain amount of persuasion. I went into May's room and started pushing her things into a plastic bag. The photograph went in first, then the Eiffel Tower, then I tried folding her dresses so that they wouldn't crease. Barry came to the door and stood watching me.

'You saw her then?' he said.

'Yes. I already told you that didn't I?'

'Yes. Of course you did.' He shifted sideways into the room, hands in his pockets. I could smell the chip fat on his clothes, his hair needed washing. 'So you don't think she'll be out for a while then?'

'No. They called the Social Services. They reckoned she was a danger to herself.'

'She is. I should think hospital is the best place for her at the moment.' He invited me to agree with his grown-up version of her situation.

'It's not, Barry. They don't understand her. It's not tablets she needs, it's the right environment.'

'Here, you mean?' The penny was beginning to drop.

'Where does she keep her shoes?' I said, using the cover of the remark to get a little closer to the door.

'You mean here, do you?' He pushed harder, then took my upper arm and clenched it tight.

'Ah, under the bed. I remember now.' I shoved his arm aside and grabbed a pair of shoes. Barry moved to block the door.

'I won't let you go,' he said.

'I'll be back. You know me.'

We stood facing each other, both of us stretched to our full heights, me a little taller than him but neither prepared to give an inch.

'Walk out of that door and I'll call the police.' Barry's background always let him down in moments of crisis. His faith in the authorities was sometimes stretched to the most ludicrous lengths.

'I'm sure they've got enough on their plates without being alerted whenever somebody leaves your cafe.'

'You're a thief. And a deserter. I'm sure they'd be interested in that.'

'All petty stuff, they couldn't give a damn.' I took a step towards him.

'Perhaps. But it might detain you for a while. I'm sure you don't want to be detained, do you?'

The harder he pushed it, the less effective his imploring became. He couldn't see it but he was making it easier for me to go, not harder. Then he made a dash into the sitting room and lunged for the phone.

'Don't be stupid, Barry.' I stood by the door; he was holding the purring receiver, his first finger poised over the 9 button. I stifled a laugh.

'I'll do it.' His voice was shaking with emotion. The situation was no longer funny. It was the end. I walked over to him and tore the phone from the wall. He held his arm over his head to protect himself. I think he thought I was going to throw it at him, instead I sent it smashing against the wall.

I said, 'Turn your pockets out.'

'What?' It was his turn to smile now. He thought I was joking.

'I said turn your fucking pockets out. Now!'

'Cliff. You only have to ask, love. How much do you want?' He scrambled to his feet and reached into his pockets.

'How much have you got?' Tormenting someone you love in cold blood is never easy. I don't think I would have been half as effective at it without my army training. But he looked at me as if I was speaking a different language.

'Here.' He fumbled a handful of coins and notes towards me. ' . . . Two years,' he whispered hoarsely, 'two years. Doesn't that mean anything to you?'

When it dies. When love dies, no words can resurrect it. And when it has died you will never know what it was that made it what it was. And for me, that was the moment it seemed to die. How was I to know it only lay sleeping?

If something won't die of natural causes sometimes you have to put it out of its misery. I landed a blow on his jaw and sent him sprawling. He scurried backwards towards the wall like a crab, cradling his jaw in his right hand.

'You want more, Barry?'

'You're crazier than she is.' His face showed something more than hurt now, something more akin to terror.

'Give me the key to the till.' He threw it over. I caught it and went downstairs while he sat curled in the corner practising his tragic face.

The till had over a hundred pounds in it. Barry hadn't cashed up for a couple of days, he was lazy like that. I took all of the notes and grabbed a handful of loose change, then locked the till again out of force of habit. I went back up to fetch May's bag and to try to say goodbye.

'I'll never trust anybody ever again.' He was wailing piteously, still on the floor. 'That's what you've done to me.' He turned his tearstained face defiantly towards me.

'Not me, Barry. You can't lay that at my door.'

'I do. I do . . . one day you'll discover the things you do actually have a bearing on the rest of the world.'

'Only if the world lets them,' I spat back.

'Why her? Why throw all of this in for her?'

'I'm all she's got,' I said in a rare moment of honesty.

'But you're all I've got.'

That one knocked me back. He wasn't frightened or angry any more, just sad. That was the moment I should have thrown it all in, apologised and asked for Barry's help to get May out. The relationship would have been fractured but it would have survived.

'It's not just her, she's not the only issue.' I'd glimpsed freedom and I couldn't turn back.

'Then tell me what the issue is and I'll do something about it.' He'd spotted a chink of hope; his eyes suddenly brightened; he wiped away snot and tears with the back of his hand.

'You wouldn't understand,' I said to my shoes.

'I would.' He struggled to his feet. 'I know everything about you, Cliff. I know what you get up to, I know who you see . . . I know what you need. You need me.'

'I don't. Anyway, I've stayed with you. I've done that now. You've had two years. That'll have to do you.'

'It's not enough.' It was a statement, not a plea.

'There is no more.' I started towards the stairs.

'That's ridiculous.' He was angry again. Another minute and I think he'd have won. I knew I had to get out of there fast.

'Look at it as two years in the bank, Barry.'

'Stay!'

'Don't follow me. Goodbye Barry.' I ran down the stairs, turning back just once as I got to the bottom. His face was crumpled like a baby's and all of the pain was haemorrhaging out. He began retching. I walked out through the cafe, closing the door on his cries, then leant against a wall and wept.

# FOUR

I HUNG AROUND the town until it got dark, then went back up to the hospital. I found May where I'd left her. She was asleep at the far end of the room, her back tight to the walls for comfort. I knocked on the glass but she didn't respond. At that moment a porter came round the corner. I asked him the way to the Gents and he pointed back in the direction I'd just come. I dropped to my knees to tie my shoelace, allowing him enough time to get out of earshot. I knocked on the glass again; May woke slowly and with effort. It took her a while to focus. I could see her mouth was dry, her eyes hooded with the strain of the drugs.

'They said I wasn't being reasonable,' she shouted through the glass. 'I don't know. I was as reasonable as I could be with a great brute of a man sticking a needle into my backside.' She stood with difficulty, then used the wall to support her to the door. I don't think she even knew who I was.

That did it. Any lingering doubts I had over getting her out of there vanished. I legged it up the corridor to the small administrative office. It was empty. A couple of coats were slung over a chair. The room was littered with empty cups and discarded chocolate wrappers. In the corner a radio was playing a Tammy Wynette song; above it there was a glass-fronted wooden cabinet with keys in it, all labelled. I found the one I needed and snatched it. When I got back to May she was still staring white-faced through the small window in the door, transfixed by a spider web of cracked plaster on the wall opposite. I opened the door and she collapsed onto me. She felt light as a feather and didn't smell too fresh.

I righted her; she swayed like a roll of carpet then found her centre of gravity. 'Did you bring my clothes?' she slurred.

I thrust the plastic bag at her, she took a step away from me, stripped her nightgown off over her head and stood stark naked in the middle of the corridor.

'May!' I cried out.

'What!' she said with equal alarm.

'Not here.' I put my jacket round her and propelled her down the corridor. I tried a few doors and then found one that gave onto a small empty side ward. There was a shower and a couple of sinks in the bathroom. I stood guard as she went in.

After fifteen minutes I was getting nervous. The chances of being caught increased as each minute passed and I knew it would be May who'd suffer the most if they did catch us. Then I heard the sound of a commotion from the direction of the nurse's room. I knocked on the bathroom door and went in. May was standing just inside the door with my jacket still round her shoulders and frozen to the spot. Her eye had been caught by a scrap of paper on the floor; she was watching it warily as if it was a snake about to spring at her. I pushed her gently beneath the shower, took my jacket from her and turned the cold tap on hard. She didn't respond immediately, but then slowly seemed to uncurl herself beneath the jet of water. She flexed her neck and bent her head back so that the water blasted her full in the face. I turned on the hot tap to make it more comfortable for her. The warmth roused her further and for the first time she seemed to become aware of my presence. She looked at me with shock and covered her breasts with her arms. I left her to it and closed the door.

She was out in five minutes looking fresh and young as though she'd spent the day walking on the prom rather than being locked in a hospital kennel. Only her eyes gave her away: pupils stretched wide and afraid, eyebrows flexing to keep focus. She'd put on her longest, thinnest dress in a delicate brown that swirled round her naked body like mist. Her wet hair was held back in an elastic band. She had no make-up on and looked more beautiful than I'd ever known. I kissed her with a passion, her face was as cold as marble. I recoiled, but she barely noticed.

We reached reception looking as much like a man and wife as we could. Her arm was wrapped tight around mine. I made a show of saying something to her and then laughing as if we'd shared a joke. But the effect I was trying to conjure up was torpedoed by the look of shock that was still plastered over her face. I thought we'd made it when the receptionist on the desk didn't look up when we passed, but just as we reached the last short corridor to the main entrance we were spotted by a male nurse.

I dropped a 'Good evening' as casually as I could, digging May in the ribs for a sociable contribution. But she was so wound up that she yelped in alarm. The nurse planted himself squarely in front of us and crossed his arms.

'What do you think you're doing?' He spoke like a policeman knowing he was about to make an arrest.

'We're going home,' I said, laughing, in a last-ditch attempt to throw him off the scent. 'Why, you're not going to try and keep us in here all night?' I laughed again, inviting May to join in but I could feel her fingernails cutting into my arm.

'You're not taking her anywhere.' His eyes travelled over her body. 'She's been Sectioned. You won't be doing her any favours.' He transferred his attention to me. I dropped May's arm from mine.

'I don't do favours,' I said. 'It's not in my line.'

'Alright then. Let's see what we can do to sort this out, shall we? Come with me and we'll have a look at the paperwork.' He waved us in the direction of reception and tried a smile but it didn't make the distance from his mouth to his eyes. I decided to brazen it out and pushed May to his left, knowing that he wouldn't be able to grab us both.

He slid three feet to the left as if he was playing British Bulldogs. 'I said we can't let you go without the paperwork.'

Behind us I could hear someone with a bleeper coming quickly towards us; the man tried to mask it but I could see the approach in his eyes. I shouted to May to run and she headed for the door. The nurse readied himself for a fair fight. I squared up to him then kicked him as hard as I could between the legs. He dropped to his knees and fell forwards clutching his balls. For the second time that day I exited to the sound of a man's tears.

# FIVE

I TOOK MAY'S arm and we zigzagged down the hill. In the idle hours of the afternoon I'd come up with the idea of hiding out on the pier for the night. One of Barry's customers worked for the security company that patrolled it and I knew he'd let us into the games arcade for a small consideration. It took us twenty minutes to get there, we hid at the approach of each siren, cowering and laughing like kids in dark doorways. We found Barry's mate, bored and smoking and leaning over the railings at the far end of the pier. He was staring at the lights on the marina and the fluorescent gulls riding the black waves. He expressed some surprise when I told him our plans but twenty quid did the trick and we were inside.

The emergency lights in the games arcade cast a strange green fog over the sleeping machines. May looked up at the huge domed ceilings and round at the garish walls as if she was walking through a dream. I found myself comforted by her presence even in the silence that lay between us. It was like that. I drew a comfort from her that I'd never really enjoyed with anybody else.

I found the power switch and turned the lights on. May stood in the centre of the room and hugged herself, turning slowly to take it all in.

'It's lovely, Cliff,' she said, wide-eyed with wonder. 'Like a palace.'

I tried to see it through her eyes but however hard I tried I couldn't.

'Can we stay?' She looked at me imploringly, clapping her hands together and jumping on the spot. I told her we could stay for as long as we wanted – at least for as long as our tame security man was on shift. She took off round the room like a child trailing an imaginary kite in the wind. She danced on her toes, occasionally pausing to scrutinise one of the machines more closely. Then an idea struck her, and she said, 'What about the machines! Can we play them?'

'Anything you want, May,' I said. 'Anything. Shall I turn them on?'

'Would you?'

'Close your eyes . . . ' I teased, 'now don't peep . . . ' I found the switch and threw it. The room burst ripely with the sound of the machines and the mechanical voices pleading for attention. May looked at me with a kind of wonder. I was flattered into believing that she held me responsible for everything she saw: for the structure of the pier that supported us above the sea, for the electricity that powered the machines, for the mechanics and electronics . . . it was pure megalomania. Her madness was beginning to reach out and touch me and I began to see some of the shadowy landmarks of May's world. I laughed like a lunatic and May took my hand and kissed it.

'And music!' I called like an impresario. 'Shall we dance!'

'Yes. Yes,' she said, then stopped and her certainty began to crumble. 'In a moment I'll wake up . . . in a moment. In a moment.'

'No, it's real, May. Look at it.' I steered her to face a machine. 'Touch it.' She reached out and touched. 'Now listen to the sea, and smell the fish and chips.' I called on her senses one by one to anchor her to the spot. 'It's real. It's all real. And it's ours for the night.'

I scampered away to find a jukebox. I jammed in a coin and immediately in the cavern of the roof I heard a needle drop heavily into the grooves of a record, then crackles and Buddy Holly singing about true love ways.

'Shall we dance?' I approached her again, hand held out in invitation. 'Like a husband and wife down for the day?'

'Yes let's.'

'Quick then, before the kiddie wakes. Can you see him?'

'Where?' She gripped my shoulder and pulled me close. I could feel her breath on my ear and her breasts on my chest. Her voice by-passed my hearing and went clean to my soul.

'Through the window,' I crooned. 'Asleep in the pram.'

'In blue?' She closed her eyes and saw him. I never knew what colour her child wore; the photo on her table was black and white and dog-eared from being held too long and too tight.

'Blue head to toe,' I said.

'And red from the sun?'

'No. We'd be careful we would. He'd have a hat. We'd think of things like that, wouldn't we?'

'Of course we would . . . hold me tighter, Cliffie. It's so cold in here.'

I wrapped my arms tight around her, but we held each other gently as though each of us was afraid to break the spell of the moment. For a while we swayed to the music. Then May said, 'Cliffie.'

'Yes.'

'I saw things this morning . . . awful things . . . everything was bad today.'

'Don't worry. You're safe now. It's alright now.'

'Sometimes it doesn't make sense. Nothing seems to make sense. I don't mind not understanding, sometimes it's best not to understand, but today when I woke up everything was clear . . . completely clear. The sun was shining and the moon was too but they were whispering, and then the clouds just came down and covered everything up like snow . . . ' Her hand knotted into a fist. I felt it clench into the small of my back.

'Quiet,' I soothed, 'just dance.'

'No. I want to tell you. You see, after that, after the clouds, then everything was bad.'

'I have days like that.'

'No you don't,' she said quickly. 'Not like this. There's Heaven and Hell and you can go from one to another by just walking across a street.'

'I know streets like that.'

'And you can find Hell in the strangest places. In some of the best people you know . . . Like you, Cliffie. Like you last night . . .'

'Look. I'm sorry. I'm sorry I hit you.'

She pulled away and looked at me with menace. The music was no longer touching her. As she stared she began swaying to a rhythm that had nothing to do with the song or the slow rocking of the waves. It was a twisting sinister beat that clawed at her neck and stretched her pupils wide. 'You hurt me, Cliffie. You hurt me, Cliffie. You hurt me . . .' The volume of her accusation grew each time she repeated it. I was afraid for her and I was afraid for myself. I no longer recognised the figure that stood before me and screamed words faster and faster until they merged into an incomprehensible wail.

'May, stop.' I took hold of her jaw and tried to stop the scream. She slapped at my arm but the noise immediately subsided. I forced her to face me. 'Listen. It's not you, May. It's the condition.'

'What's the difference? I wish somebody would tell me what the difference was then I wouldn't feel so scared.' Suddenly she snapped round; I thought somebody had come into the room without my noticing. 'He's crying,' she said, making for the door. I grabbed at her arm to prevent her from leaving.

'I can't hear him,' I said, but I could, don't ask me how but I could hear the plaintive cry of a child screaming against the wind.

'Listen,' she implored. 'Just above the waves.'

'He wouldn't cry,' I pleaded. 'Not ours. He'd be as good as gold.' I knew that the more real the child became, the worse it would be for both of us.

'Then they must be taking him away from me!' She tugged her arm free and ran for the fire exit. Above the sound of the sea I could hear the rain pelting on the roof and the wind gusting at the windows. I caught her just before she got the door open.

'Don't . . . you'll catch your death out there.'

'But I have to go to him.' She was frantic, lost in a scene from her past. She had only once opened the door on that particular nightmare. It was the afternoon we had made furtive love in her room and then lain naked on her bed. She had traced the contours of her belly with her fingernails and told me that once she had had a child. She laid the dog-eared photo on her naked breast as she talked. The child, it seemed, had been taken away and given away to a couple who had a greater need for it.

I struck her face. I knew she would hate me for it but I had no other option. 'Stop, May. Stop it now.'

'Please let me go.'

'No. Stop.'

The crying stopped.

'Gone,' she said. 'Again.'

'He was never there, love,' I lied.

'He was. He was.'

I released her arm. She drifted off into the shadows; the machines continued to torture the silence. I went over and switched them off, then turned off the main lights so that the room fell back into green darkness.

Some places should always be experienced in the dark. The pier is one of them; the shadows make a different sense of the space and give it a meaning that's altogether more human. The darkness allows you to take a slice of the room and own it for a moment before passing on and finding another and another until all of the room is yours. May was alone too in the shadows. I didn't want to disturb her, I wanted her to come and find me when she felt ready. I sat on the floor and lit a cigarette. After a while I could make out her shape as she moved by the wall on the far side of the room; she could have been watching me too but it was hard to tell. Then she came over and sat down beside me, her face found my shoulder and I put my arm round her.

'That's nice,' she said, quiet now. 'Just like that. Don't let go.'

'I won't.'

'Am I crazy, Cliffie?'

'Sometimes.'

'Does it matter to you?'

'Only because it matters to you.'

'What will we do?'

'What do you want? I'll do what you want to do.' I craned my neck to look at her face.

'I want you to stay with me until I tell you not to.'

'I'll stay as long as you like.'

'You have to promise.'

'Cross my heart.'

She sighed, 'With you nothing seems so bad. I just can't stand being alone.'

We remained like that for a while. Once or twice I drifted off into a fractured sleep then awoke with May still against me, her breathing still shallow and fast. Occasionally she twitched so violently it nearly threw me off her but she clung on.

'How about the machines?' I said eventually.

'Whatever you like, Cliffie.'

'Shall we play them?'

'Could we?'

'Of course we could.' I scouted around and found a heavy old ashtray on a metal stand. I lobbed it at the pay booth to shatter the glass.

We played the machines with stolen coins and little enthusiasm. May was distracted, she claimed to hear voices but I reassured her that it was just the wind finding its way through the cracks in the windows. Finally we stopped and I fell asleep with May watching over me.

# SIX

WHEN MAY NUDGED me awake it was dawn, and the storm had blown itself out. The arcade looked like hell in the daylight; broken glass was scattered like frost among the machines. May had tried to clear it up while I slept but she'd cut her hand and stained the carpet with her blood. Looking round the room, it was hard to tie up the scale of the destruction with what I remembered about the night before. For the state that place was in, the madness must have gone far deeper than I remembered.

I knew we had to get out before the security guard came in and discovered what we'd done. It meant the sack for him whatever happened, but I didn't linger on the guilt, I was more concerned about Hollister. Hollister was one of Barry's gangster friends; he had shares in the pier and a number of properties around the town and wasn't averse to getting his way with a bit of physical violence. He liked to cultivate what he considered to be an upmarket image by wearing flashy suits and lots of heavy gold jewellery but he was a thug who could never hide his roots no matter how hard he tried. I didn't much fancy our chances if Hollister reached us before the law did.

We crept out of the fire exit and off the pier then crossed the prom and went to the all-night cafe opposite the vegetable market for breakfast.

'Two teas and two rounds of toast,' I said to the bored girl behind the counter. 'Toast suit you, May?'

'I'm not hungry.' May was a mess, she didn't seem to know where she was or what the hell was going on.

'She'll have the toast,' I answered for her. 'Bring it over, will you.' We took a seat by the steamed window. It was just after six but the place was full. In the background a radio was playing an old Kinks song.

I lit two cigarettes and gave one to May. She looked at it as if it was the first one she'd seen before clamping it between her lips and drawing hard. The Kinks segued to the local news and from the first report it was clear that either the hospital or Barry had called in the police. May was caricatured as an escaped lunatic, I was a thug who'd masterminded her escape.

'That's it then,' May said flatly. I saw the girl at the counter staring over at us as it dawned on her who we were.

'Course it isn't,' I chivvied. 'They've got to find us first . . . Funny how the press always stoops to a caricature isn't it? The dangerous and the insane. It's like the army in that respect: he's fat, he's lazy, he farts in his sleep. That's how they get a handle on you, no respect for your finer feelings.'

'You were in the army, Cliffie?' Her interest perked up even though I'd bored her with tales of my career as a squaddie many times before.

'Yeah. I left when the war came and they called us back from leave. I told a sergeant I was handing in my notice, "Like How'syourfather you are," he said. "There's no getting out for you, Sonny Jim, we're going to the South Atlantic, there's a conflict on. Haven't you read the newspapers?" Course I'd read the papers. "I'm an educated man," I said. "That's why I'm resigning. I didn't join the army to fight. That was never in the job description" . . . Anyway, I deserted, changed my name and ended up at Barry's . . . '

May was chewing her lip, I could see she wasn't really listening to what I was telling her. She said, 'I don't feel so good. Not right at all.' Her eyes were flicking around the room. She fidgeted with her cigarette then lit another from the stub. 'I need my tablets.'

'You're hungry, that's all. A good square meal inside you and you'll be on top of the world.' It was clear that May needed help, not food, but by then I'd run out of ideas.

'I didn't sleep a wink last night,' she said, throwing some of the blame towards me.

'Didn't you? I slept like a baby. Excitement always takes me like that.'

'That's two days. That's how it gets you. You don't sleep. Your head starts buzzing. No sleep and you start to burn. Everything inside you starts to burn. No sleep and you start going faster and faster. Like running down a steep hill. Faster and faster . . . and soon you can't stop. Then you don't want to stop. Then . . . '

The girl brought the toast over. She was in her late teens, insolent and bored. She had a supermodel figure, a T-shaped face and a mane of bleached blonde hair. She was over six feet tall in shrink-fit Levi's and platform soles. Barry would have had something to say about her attitude. He always reckoned it was a mark of class to be able to serve people without diminishing either yourself or those you were serving. But the girl looked at us as though we were a pair of freaks. Neither of us had any inclination to tell her where to go so we just stared back. She threw the plates on the table and stalked off.

'Cow,' May said, loud enough for her to hear but without any real spirit.

'Say something, did you?' The girl spun round, itching for a row.

'Leave it,' I implored. 'Don't cause a scene. I'll get your tablets. Just leave it.'

'I said cow,' May said. The girl came back towards us. I don't know what she had in mind but, whatever it was, as soon as she saw May's eyes her anger diluted to a look of pity.

'Cow,' May said again, this time without conviction, then buried her head in her arms and wept.

'This down to you is it?' the waitress said to me, then slid onto the bench beside May and put her arm round her.

'Nothing to do with me,' I said.

'Men.' The girl began massaging May's shoulders and soothing her with quiet careful words. I watched her respond first to the tenderness, then to the words. Soon she was wiping away the last of her tears and apologising to us both.

'It was you – on the news – wasn't it?' The girl looked to me to confirm her suspicions. I did. She said, 'You don't look dangerous to me.'

'It's still early in the day,' I said glibly.

'You won't get far. I don't suppose you've got a car.'

'I can get one.' I was already resenting her interference. May was my responsibility, nobody else's.

'If you're sure.' She picked up on my hostility.

'But you could . . . I mean, I've got to go and fetch something. Maybe you could keep an . . . maybe May could stay here for a while.'

'I'll take care of her,' the girl said.

'Thanks. I'll be back as soon as I can.' I leant down and kissed May on her cheek. I had a premonition that I wouldn't see her again. But it was another parting I was foreseeing, a much more painful parting. 'Thanks,' I said again to the girl and went out past a bus crew tucking into their fry ups.

Outside the town was waking to another loveless morning. I knew there were some of May's tablets at Barry's but I didn't relish the prospect of seeing him again. I'd left my keys behind the day before which made a confrontation inevitable. The one small hope I clung onto was that I could sneak in round the back while he was tied up serving the early regulars in the cafe.

I reached the cafe with a sinking heart. The shutters were still drawn and a crate of milk was turning to sludge in the heat of the rising sun. Last night's litter made the doorstep look like a dosser's bedroom. I went round the alleyway to the back door in the hope that Barry had forgotten to lock up. When I tried the handle the door was yanked open and I fell at his feet.

'Cliff,' he said, snarling my name. 'How nice to see you. Why don't you come in.'

I tailed Barry upstairs. 'I'm not staying,' I started to explain, 'I'm here on an errand. I have to fetch May's tablets.' I thought it best not to raise his hopes of a reunion.

Barry stopped at the top. 'Why don't you come in and say hello to Mr Hollister.'

'No thanks.' The shock of his name struck me like a fist in the face. I could smell Hollister's stale, sweet scent from the hallway. It looked like the half hour I'd dawdled away getting to the cafe could have ended up costing us our liberty. Even so, I was surprised that Hollister had responded so quickly. Some time later I discovered that the security man had gone straight to his flat in the hope of saving his neck. Unfortunately for him it didn't turn out that way.

'Look Barry.' I took his arm, and he winced at the contact. 'It's over. Right?' I was whispering now in the hope that Hollister hadn't heard me come in. 'Now tell Hollister I'm sorry I missed him but I sent him my love, alright?' I kissed Barry on the lips. It was a betrayer's kiss and he knew it.

'Why not tell him yourself?'

I felt a pair of hands grab me from behind and push me into the living room. I twisted round to see one of Hollister's leather-jacketed donkeys glaring. I fell into the room to be confronted by the man himself dripping gold jewellery over the cat. He'd put on weight since I'd seen him last, he seemed paler, his skin almost transparent, his jowls folding like pastry over the pristine white collar of his shirt. He was wearing an expensive blue double-breasted suit with a pink carnation in his button hole, and someone had teased the last few strands of ginger hair into something resembling ploughlines over his domed scalp. But his eyes were the same: rheumy and powder blue, set in pools of bloody Mary like somebody who'd taken a face full of teargas. Hollister without his shades on was a sight to behold.

'Clifford!' He sprung to life with a showy pretence of animation that didn't suit his features. But it was clear that he wasn't expecting me. 'My my, what a surprise. We were just discussing you, weren't we, Barry? A fugitive. Think of that. I always said you'd make something of yourself.'

'I'm sorry Mr Hollister,' I said with undue deference, 'I can't stay. I've come on an errand for May.'

'Yes. May. I have to say that when Barry told me it was her I was surprised at you. I've always imagined your tastes to be a little more . . . ' he reached for the word ' . . . exotic.' He smiled. When Hollister was in his amateur dramatics mode it was best to go along with him.

'She needed help,' I said.

'I hope she fucks, Clifford.' The shutters came down over his eyes. 'I couldn't imagine any other reason to throw in my lot with a lunatic.' He coughed loudly and productively then spat into his silk handkerchief. He examined what he had produced before folding it into the blue square and returning it to his pocket. The action seemed to have rid him of his bile, and his show of good humour returned. He patted the settee beside him and motioned for me to join him.

'I'm sorry,' I tried one last time. 'I really have to go.' The black shadow of Hollister's donkey came quickly up behind me. From the corner of my eye I saw a gloved hand lash out and felt a sharp striking pain in my kidneys. As I dropped towards the floor a steel-capped boot came up to meet me half way. When I hit the floor I writhed as if I'd been skewered on a lance. The boot threatened more but Hollister called it off then cleared Barry and his thug from the room. He watched as I fought for breath, then when my head stopped singing and I tried to struggle up he tenderly helped me to a chair.

'Nasty business,' he said with regret, disclaiming all responsibility. 'Nasty brutish behaviour. Here, you've cut your lip.' He passed me a handkerchief. I wiped my lip with it, in my daze remembering too late the contents. A muscular ball of mucus appended itself like a leech to my face. Hollister watched as I tried to remove it.

'That's better.' He looked me up and down, removing the last elastic trace with his fingernail. 'Much better . . . now, we have matters to discuss, don't we.'

'Yes,' I said hoarsely.

'I anticipated you'd return here. But not quite so soon, I have to say.'

'Like a bad penny eh?'

'A return to the scene of the crime perhaps. Desertion is a crime.

At least that's how we view it in our circle. But then we're old-fashioned. You know us, don't you.'

'Conservative values, Mr Hollister. Yes, I know you.'

Close to, I could see how hard he was trying to stay in control. Much of his anger seemed to be going into the rubbing motion he was employing on the cat's back. The cat, which had sprung back to his knee at the earliest opportunity, was enjoying every minute of it.

'But as if leaving one of my closest friends broken-hearted wasn't enough, you then choose to wreak havoc on my premises without, I imagine, any intention of paying for the damage. And please don't ask me for credit as refusal often offends.'

Hollister seized the cat's jaw in his right hand and, with the other holding its front legs, twisted it sharply sideways. The cat screeched in alarm before fighting clear of his grasp. It staggered away flexing its neck.

'Could you . . . ' I started tentatively, 'I mean, could you put a figure on the damage?'

'It's a little early to tell. The full extent has yet to be assessed, but initial estimates suggest a broken till, two pin tables, fifty pounds in cash, one night's lodgings . . . and the price of severe discomfiture for poor Alan.'

'Alan?'

'Our former security man. He fell and hurt himself – his face, or his hands, I don't know. I haven't quite decided yet . . . perhaps it should be his eyes. A blind night watchman. That has a certain ring to it, don't you think?'

He was pushing his gangster act a little far for my liking. I knew Hollister was capable of gross unpleasantness but I'd never considered him to be a proper first division villain. He had too much intelligence for that. Pure villainy requires a good deal less imagination than he was capable of showing and a deal more mental instability. The Krays, to quote a popular example, maintained their status by quite brutal exhibitions of entirely unpredictable violence. Hollister finally plucked the figure from thin air. 'Call it two thousand pounds . . . does that seem reasonable?' He knew it might just as well have been two hundred thousand, that amount of cash was way out of my reach.

'Tell you what,' I floated, 'give me a couple of days. I'll put the matter into the hands of my accountants. Now, if you'll excuse me I really should go.' I pictured May waiting in the cafe; her paranoia running riot as the place filled up. If I left it too long she'd be gone.

'Go?'

'Yes. I'm pushed for time.'

'Do be realistic, just how far do you think you can get?'

'Far enough.'

'I doubt it. By now the police will have circulated your description.'

'I'm sure they've got bigger rogues to fry than me.'

He was taken aback. 'You're a rank amateur at law breaking, aren't you?' I shrugged. 'If you must indulge in criminal activities do so discreetly. Rule Two. Rule One of course is, strike against those incapable of fighting back.'

I egged him on. 'Oh, I always was discreet.'

'No, discretion requires that one must not offend against respectability. The statute books, after all, are little more than a codification of the moral consensus. Let everything be tried against the greatest good of the greatest number of people. Be utilitarian in your misdemeanours.'

I suddenly knew that it was going to be alright. Hollister was beginning to enjoy himself. After all he had a captive audience. I knew he'd always quite liked me. Alone among Barry's circle I think he knew what made me tick.

'Look.' I decided to make one last bid for freedom. 'It's very kind of you to show such an interest in my wellbeing, Mr Hollister. And I'd love to stay but . . . '

'Fraud yes . . . ' He was in full flow and wasn't about to be diverted from his lecture. 'Make a mental note. Fraud is acceptable, we all indulge in fraud – even the people who police it. In common with drug abuse, legislation exists solely to protect the market. Murder: murder . . . perhaps, if the ends justify the means. Rape, certainly not. And theft, well, here we come to the case in point. Personal property is sacrosanct, is it not.'

'I wouldn't know. I don't own any.'

He seemed to be weighing up his options. He spread his thick hand over his mouth then stroked it downwards. 'When the police have finished with you I'll be waiting. I'm prepared to give you a few months to amass what you owe me. And when you have repaid your debt to society you can then repay your debt to me . . . You look concerned. Why? You surely acknowledge the fact that you simply can't keep taking without at some stage being called upon to repay your debts.'

'I've never taken anything that anybody really wanted.'

'A poor justification. And should you intend to use it in your defence I'd recommend engaging an imaginative brief.'

I stood, trying my luck. 'That's how I live. Take it or leave it . . . but I really have to go.'

'All right, Clifford. I don't mind a little sport. If you can get out of here without our friend in the leather jacket stopping you then you're quite free to go. If he does catch you then I'm afraid you'll be at his mercy. But I won't call him . . . not until I've counted to twenty anyway.'

He smiled, remaining seated, and patted my leg.

'One,' he said, then continued the count. As I got to the door he'd reached five. By the time I'd seen that his thug was in the back room talking to Barry he'd reached ten. I tore into May's room, grabbed her tablets then fled from the cafe.

# SEVEN

THERE WASN'T MUCH pain, I just had the nagging suspicion that the sharp ache in my kidneys might signal something needing attention. But the priority was to get out of town before either Hollister or the law caught up with us. So, after collecting May from the cafe, we walked north through the busying streets; silent, weighed down by the baggage of the previous day. Finally, May broke the silence by asking where we were going.

'Away. Anywhere.' I had to admit that I hadn't given a great deal of thought to the question. Until then, I'd always travelled alone and destinations had never been that important.

'Wait!' May stopped suddenly and dropped to her knees in the middle of the pavement. Brushing back the hair that fell over her face, she began rummaging through one of the plastic bags. She pulled out a dress and frisked it, coming up with a bundle of letters from the side pocket. 'Here!' She clutched the letters to her heart. 'We can go here!' She stripped an old tattered envelope from the elastic-banded wad of mail and held it out to me. The name and stamp had been torn off, but scrawled in a spidery hand, I could make out a north London post code. 'See?' she said. 'It was all meant to happen. I forgot. This is where we have to go.'

'Whose address is it?'

'Just a friend,' May said coyly. 'Somewhere I used to be.'

I didn't hold out much hope, but at least it provided us with that elusive destination. 'I'll get us a car,' I said.

'How? We haven't got any money have we?'

'Brute force and a passing acquaintance with the workings of the internal combustion engine. What colour?'

'Red.'

'Right.'

'No. Green.'

We were on a main shopping street, the traffic heavy around us, so we took a narrow side street to the car parks behind the stores and searched out a green car there. May kept watch while I broke the window. I had the engine going within a minute and soon we were sailing off up London Road and out of town. May laughed gleefully in the passenger seat, waving regally to the people we passed. But as we left the town behind, she fell silent again.

Ten minutes passed, punctuated by her sighs, then she said, 'It's dead. It's all dead.'

I said, 'What's that?' as lightly as I could to an opener like that.

'Me. Everything I mean. Everything I am. Whatever happened to the summer?'

'It's here. Look all around you.'

'I wish it would rain.'

And so it went on until she'd driven me half crazy with her misery. Then I offered her something else by asking her for more details about the address on the envelope.

'I can't. Not yet. You'll see.' She looked slyly at me.

'Man or woman?'

'Woman.'

'Tell me something about her. Anything.'

'Oh, she's old, tired, sad. But she keeps a clean house.' With a smile on her face, she drifted off into her memories, and I left her to them. At least there, like a dog chained to the railings, she was safe for a while. Then her smile slipped again and she began fractiously chewing her thumbnail. Anxiety twisted her face into a scowl.

'She's a friend then?' I said, trying to divert her back onto the rails of happiness.

'Oh yes, a friend,' she said enthusiastically.

'Have you known her long?'

'Ages.'

'And we'll be welcome?'

'Oh yes.'

'Are you sure?'

'There'll be tears,' she said, 'recriminations. But underneath she'll be happy.'

'Emotional then?' I was becoming interested in the woman, half beginning to believe that she was real after all.

'A woman. That's all. At the mercy of men in a man's world. Life dealt her a losing hand.'

'Well, there's something we'll have in common.'

'Somebody loved you once.'

'Me? No, May, I bear all the scars of a childhood starved of affection: a penchant for buxom women and an aversion to solitude.'

'I loved you, Cliffie.'

'Loved?' The change in tense started alarm bells ringing.

'Yes. Loved. Because love doesn't begin at the beginning and end with the parting. It goes deeper than that.'

'How?'

'It can. I know it can. Love can heal,' she said with certainty. 'And when it heals then it goes deeper.' She pulled the sun visor down and took a look at herself in the mirror. Then she found her make-up bag and powdered her face.

'Why do you do that?' I said. 'It makes you look like a ghost.'

'I am a ghost.'

'Oh Christ, May, give it a rest. Give us both a break.'

Ignoring me, she plastered on a gash of bright red lipstick which, along with the powder, had the effect of making her look like a corpse that had been dragged from a river. She seemed pleased with the effect. I transferred my attention to the old-fashioned dials that were monitoring the vital functions of the car. The petrol gauge had dropped from a quarter full to the reserve band in less than a mile.

I said, 'We need to find a garage.'

'Where's the baby?' May wasn't interested in the practicalities of our escape, she was back on the pier.

'He's here.' Sometimes it was easier to go along with her.

'He wasn't taken from me then?'

'From you? No chance. He's here – in the back.'

'Where?' She craned her neck.

'No. Don't look round. He's here. Believe me.'

'And the day. Will he remember it?'

'It'll be his first memory . . . You and me and the sun and the sea.'

She began to cry; gentle, despairing tears. 'Is he beautiful?'

'Is he?' I threw back.

'Yes . . . I wish he was real.'

'Maybe he's as real as your pain.' I wanted to hurt her. To sting her from self pity.

'You don't understand or you wouldn't say that!' She punched me heavily on the shoulder. The car slewed on the dual-carriageway. Almost immediately the fuel light began to flash on the dashboard and the car started kicking beneath us. Ahead, lying along a bend on the road, there was a row of medium-sized cottages and a village school. I pulled off the dual-carriageway and into the lay-by outside the school.

The playground was full of children in red sweatshirts running with tiny explosions of purpose that sent them scattering and regrouping within the wire. May, wiping her tears, her anger quickly forgotten, was transfixed. She watched the children as if she was looking at a roomful of jewels. Then she saw something else and it took me a second to realise what had caught her attention. It was a blue Volvo estate car, parked at the front of the row of vehicles on the lay-by. May let herself out and went up to the other car. She peered into the back window, then I got out too and saw that she was staring at a child's safety seat. I knew what she was thinking momentarily before she did.

'People shouldn't leave children like that,' she said when I reached her. 'It's not fair.'

'He's asleep. His mother's probably just nipped into the school.' I took her gently by the arm to try and steer her away. A woman at the school gate was watching us. I saw her look towards the playground. She was clearly not the mother of the child in the car but she was searching her out. 'Come on, May. Time to go.' I exerted a little more pressure on her arm. She shrugged me off with a thrash of her shoulder. Then she tried the back door of the car. It swung open. The woman at the school gate froze, she was caught between coming after us and alerting a mother that she was just about to lose her baby. At that moment I heard a cry from within the shadows of the school building, the mother was fighting frantically to push her way through the mass of red in the playground. She was a well-dressed woman in a short linen jacket. You could see she had money and the sort of velvet life that cushioned her from the grimmer aspects of the world. Otherwise why should she have left a child in an unlocked car and the keys in the ignition? I watched her with a grim fascination as, white with panic, she tried to fight free of the kids.

'May, come away now!' I tried to pull her from the car, but I knew that the offence had been committed the moment she had been spotted opening the door. Whatever had gone before, at the hospital and on the pier, would pale by comparison with the attempted kidnap of a child.

I tried to drag May from the car one last time but by then she'd somehow released the baby from the seat harness. It was waking and beginning to cry weakly. The woman had reached the school gate but in her haste she was fumbling with the catch. May slipped onto the back seat and bounced the child gently on her knees.

'Drive, Cliffie. Come on, let's go.' The woman was close now, she was flushed and angry and afraid. I could see she'd clenched her hands into tight fists. She was young and attractive; a natural blonde in dark trousers and an expensive blouse. She was pleading to me with her cover girl eyes. I wanted to shout to her, to say something that would allay her fears. But I knew whatever I said would sound ludicrous so I waved instead as I skirted the car and dived into the driver's seat. We were out onto the road just before she got her hands on the back door handle. May didn't even look round. I watched the woman diminish in the rearview mirror, frozen to the spot, clutching her arms to her empty breast and beginning to cry hysterically. A posse of other mothers was soon around her. It was clear that she couldn't believe what had happened to her. I knew how she was feeling.

# EIGHT

MAY FREE-FELL joyously into madness. I watched her in the mirror cooing at the child with a crazed tenderness. Wisdom seemed to be passing between them but it was seeping upwards from the child to the mother who was learning with each uttered syllable what lay ahead of her once her innocence was gone.

'You were like this once,' she said.

'Not me. Never me.' Something about our predicament took me back to the sense of powerlessness at the beginning of it all. 'They'll lock us up now. You know that.'

'Not if we keep running.'

'We couldn't run far or fast enough.'

May began rubbing the child's face with the crook of her finger. Its mouth opened, anticipating the firm nub of a nipple. As she teased it with her little finger, the tiny moist parting closed over it and suckled. The pearls of its blue eyes looked trustingly into hers. May looked deep into them and said, 'I've been running for too long already.'

I reckoned we didn't have much time before the machinery of penal retribution was fired up and set chugging after us. We had to find somewhere to hide, after that we could talk about getting the child back to its mother.

I turned up the exit ramp and left the dual-carriageway. At the next roundabout I followed the signs towards a town and was soon heading for the mess of buildings that marked the outskirts.

Temporary signposts pointed the way down an unmade road to a new estate. House shells sprawled over the crust of a flattened forest. The few parched trees that had survived the onslaught were white with concrete dust.

'This should do,' I said to the face in the mirror as we blazed a trail of dust along the dirt track.

'Fine. It looks lovely.'

'It's not lovely May, it's a building site . . . just a fucking building site.'

'Cliffie. Language!' She gestured to the lump on her lap which had started grunting as it voided itself into its nappy.

'Why did you do it?'

'Don't be cross with me.'

'I am cross with you. It was stupid.'

'I know. But it won't be for long, will it? Then we can give it back.' She smiled at me and I forgave her.

One road led to another, then we arrived at a cul-de-sac of large executive properties. The wooden frame of the corner house had already been clad in bricks and plaster; all it now needed was its coat of white paint and mock Tudor woodwork. A doorless double garage protruded from the side and a sign on stilts hammered into the front lawn proclaimed it to be a 'Show Home for a New Generation'.

I drove up the drive and forced the car into a stack of plasterboard propped up against the back wall of the garage. Work was progressing on a far corner of the estate; a cloud of dust and diesel smoke floated towards us on the gentle breeze.

'Are we home?' May said, waiting to be let out of the back seat.

'We're home.' I got out of the car and opened May's door for her. She struggled out, waddling to her feet but unwilling to relinquish the burden of the bundled child. I said, 'We'll stay here for a while. Until . . . '

'Yes,' May cut in sharply. 'I know, Cliffie. I know. Until we have to go.'

The house was more complete than the outside had promised. The floors had been concreted, the glaziers had been in and there was water to a brass tap on a copper pipe that leaned precariously over a filthy rubber bucket in a corner of the kitchen. May nosed into each of the generously proportioned rooms, staking out her territory. 'We need food and nappies,' she said when we met up again in the lounge.

'Or just food and I take the baby back.'

'Alright . . . alright! I will when it's time. But not yet. Just give me some time. Please.'

'Yes. Alright.'

'And you won't mention it again?'

'No.'

At the time it seemed a reasonable trade off. After all, May had nothing, the county woman seemingly everything. That's how I argued it to myself and I knew the logic would hold water like a leaking bucket for an hour or so.

Time dragged towards midday. May had miraculously fallen asleep with the baby content on her lap. She lay slouched, at peace, on a makeshift bed of empty cement bags and wooden pallets. We'd found a pile of shopping in the back of the Volvo and, within it, a shrink-wrapped parcel of plastic nappies. The first efforts at securing them lay strewn around the room, by the fourth we'd managed to master the peculiar system of double-sided tape and elasticated legs and the baby – now transformed from a sexless lump into a boy of around six months – had lost the game of air football and been securely trussed into its plastic wrapping.

I watched them sleep and for a while considered taking the child from her. But May needed the rest and I knew she'd probably wake if I disturbed her. The tension seemed to have gone from her face; the child twitched on her chest, sniffling and sucking its fingers. They moved in unison, perfectly content to borrow each other's warmth. I wandered up the bare wooden stairs and looked out over the site. I was fairly sure we hadn't been seen when we drove off the main road, so I relaxed and smoked, trying not to think about later, but instead ended up playing the familiar game of reviewing the past.

Since I was young the past has had a tendency to creep up in moments of quiet and busy itself like a wayward child, scampering around the unguarded moments of the present. As it arrived I found myself in the thin brown room with its smell of old newspapers and second-hand furniture and a deep chill that caused the air to bunch and billow as I breathed. The angles of light through the netted window and the scale of the bed marked the time as long before; some time before the institution; a time and place resonant with meaning and menace.

I know little about my early life. The past was a commodity closely guarded by the authorities at the home. Whenever I asked about my parents my questions were met by vague assurances that the information was on file and that I'd be made party to it when I was old enough. I learnt from a matron who took a shine to me that I was three years old when I first arrived at the home. The thin brown room comes from before then. But the memory of it is scorched deep: the scene viewed from beneath a tall bed (a remembered place of safety; dark, cold and lonely but safe). A solitary game in an attic room. Imaginary friends, the only friends I had. A teddy bear, an old ball of wool and a tin soldier. Then, a presence sensed in the hallway, confirmed by creaking floorboards, prompting a scurrying beneath the bed. The door snatched open, cracking the wall. A man's voice, thick and beery, and a woman pushed before him into the room. The woman losing her footing, falling heavily onto the bed. The man becoming thighs, then knees and then feet as he too approaches. Muffled sighs of pain and a rhythmic creaking.

And then I am discovered because I am singing beneath the bed: three blind mice, three blind mice, see how they run; a song taught at my mother's knee in a rare moment of intimacy. I sing the song because it blocks my mother's screams from my ears. I sing the song because I hope she will hear it and feel safe, knowing that I am beneath the bed and ready to come if she calls me. But it is the man's face that is thrust into my dark space – with large bloodshot eyes, pale tight skin, grim sneering mouth. I feel my arm nearly torn from its socket and then I am outside the room and the door is kicked shut. Not long after that (it could have been a day, it could have been a year – the memories have been sewn together) a car arrives and a woman leads me into it. She wears a strange flat red beret and a macintosh coat and allows me to operate the traffic indicators. I remember the journey through the town and into the open spaces of the country.

The countryside is unfamiliar, as are the tall metal gates that we drive through. All the way there I imagine I am being punished for hiding beneath the bed. All the way there I know that if I had not sung the song then my mother would not have made me leave. But she did. And that's how I arrived at the place that was to become my home until I escaped when I was sixteen.

'Cliffie?' May is behind me. I have not heard her come up the stairs.

'Hello.'

'How long did I sleep?'

I look at the time, glad to be facing away from her. Glad not to be seeing her through the salt of old tears. 'An hour, just an hour.' I hear her come further into the room; tentative, wondering why I do not turn to face her.

'What's the matter, Cliffie?'

'Nothing.'

'There is. Tell me . . . Come here.' She holds her arms wide and I collapse into them sobbing so violently that I can barely speak. I abandon myself to the wave of pain and let it wash over me. The tears sting like acid as they burn down my cheeks to soak the shoulder of her thin dress. May says nothing. She just bears my weight on her shoulders. But, as always, the tears achieve nothing beyond indicating the vast reservoir that is inside me. Then, in the calm that follows, the child's waking tears draw us both back downstairs and May lifts another infant to her breast.

'You see,' she says, rocking the child silent.

'What?'

'I can do it. I can look after him.'

'I never doubted you could.'

'You did. Look at me. You did.'

I look at her. I did. 'Does it matter what I thought?'

'Yes it does. You know it does.'

'Yes . . . so I take him back now?'

She held him out to me like a beggar on the take. He looked

confused as he was passed through the space between us, but content again as he found another shoulder to lean on. Then we both heard it: something coming from the forest; loud and thudding expensively overhead.

'Helicopter,' I said unnecessarily.

'Can they see the car?'

'I doubt it. Keep away from the window.'

The helicopter circled low a couple of times then took off in the direction of the town.

'No. We're safe,' I said.

'You'd better go.' She patted the child's head with detached interest. 'Go on. I'll be alright.' Her mood had lifted. For the first time since the hospital I saw some of the old May coming through.

'I won't take the car.'

'No.'

'I'll go through the trees and leave him somewhere he'll be found.' Now it was time to go I realised I was looking for excuses to stay. The domesticity, however contrived and unreal, was comforting.

May said, 'Bring some food if you can.'

I struck out through the tangled edge of the forest, clutching the child tightly to my shoulder. His head bobbed unsteadily on a weak neck as he peered around him, fixing on the flashes of sky through the dense branches. I started talking to him, pointing things out. He responded by smiling and I could see how children weave their spell over you. Then we were through the forest and at the edge of a sixties development of squat houses with scaffolding-pole porches and overgrown grass verges scored deep with tyre tracks. I walked past a long row of garages and came to a rudimentary precinct with an orange and yellow convenience store, a betting shop and a closed and boarded-up greengrocer's. It was lunchtime but the place seemed curiously unlived-in; it was a breeding ground for despair. There were no churches or pubs, just row upon row of small brick-built hovels leaning together in twos for support and to save space. The ones with tended gardens just served to make the road look even worse.

I finally came across a house with a number of pushchairs and empty prams outside and laid the baby in one of the prams. He waved into the air as I put him down. On an impulse I leant down and kissed him. Then I hurried away, past the front window where I could see a group of women drinking tea and smoking cigarettes. By the law of averages it seemed unlikely that the child would be snatched twice in one day.

At the precinct I bought some bread, cheese and a bottle of wine. Then I made my way back through the forest to May, waiting for me in the show home for a new generation.

# NINE

WE SPENT THE rest of the day in different rooms; silent, brooding, kicking our heels with the vague expectation of a knock on the door. But none came. The loss of the child left a vacuum in the house that neither of us could fill. Each hour, on the hour, I went down to the car and listened to the local news. It wasn't until four o'clock that they reported the discovery of the child in the pram. They ran an interview with an excitable woman from the estate; the mother was not referred to. I waited for some mention of the search in the hope it would give us a clue as to whether we should move on but they gave out the usual line about the police pursuing their enquiries. The night finally came.

I think we both knew that the end was coming. The truth was that we'd known it from the moment we left the hospital, but neither of us was ready to confront it. So we continued wandering round the house like a pair of newlyweds unable to believe our good fortune at being able to afford such a prestige property.

The estate had fallen silent long before dusk. I watched from the bedroom as the strip of orange over the forest was compressed to nothing by the weight of the grey sky. May came in with her arms crossed and leant against the wall, staring out of the window.

'Hungry?' I asked her for want of something to say.

'Not really.'

'How are you feeling?'

'Better . . . a bit better I think.'

'We ought to leave soon and get rid of the car.'

'Whatever you think.'

'Maybe I'll fetch some hot food.'

'That would be nice.'

'I don't know. They'll be keeping an eye out for us by now.'

'Oh,' she said neutrally. I lit two cigarettes and gave one to her. The nicotine was sustaining us.

'I hate the night, Cliffie, don't you?'

'I don't mind it.'

'It's not safe.'

'That depends, doesn't it.'

'On what?'

'On who you're with.'

By now, the room was almost black. Behind the trees was the sodium dome of the suburb. May came up and took my arm. She'd washed off her make-up and put on some fresh perfume. It was soft and quiet and unlike the stuff she usually used.

'It's beautiful, isn't it,' she said.

'What?'

'Being on the inside with someone.'

'It's good being with you.'

'Do you mean that?'

'You know I do.'

'I thought it was just me.'

'Course not. Why do you think I'm here?'

'I don't know,' she said. 'I'd like to think it was because you wanted to be.'

'I don't do anything I don't want,' I said, but in saying it I realised with a jolt that it was a claim I could no longer make. I'd taken the Volvo against my will and I'd considered taking the child from her against my will and hers. The burden of responsibility towards her was forcing compromises and causing a faint stirring of something. I think it was loyalty, or perhaps it was just guilt.

My mind went back to Barry. I wondered what he'd be thinking that night. I knew he wouldn't sleep with the worry of it all. He was a martyr to insomnia; some nights I'd keep him company until dawn.

Then, with the demons gone, we'd fall asleep in each other's arms on the settee. Sometimes we'd wake and make love in the unfamiliar setting. The nights we shared like that were among the best we had; neither of us pretending; neither of us trying to hide the need for each other with stupid games.

I pictured him in the wicker chair with only the cat for company. He wouldn't have bothered putting the lights on but would be staring up the street; watching the couples wander from restaurant window to restaurant window before choosing where to eat; the groups spilling from the pubs, horsing around, happy and inebriated. It was a habit he had, watching the world go by while he sipped his camomile tea. If I cry now it's because I wonder how he put up with me for as long as he did. He deserved better.

'What are you thinking?' May said.

'I was thinking about Barry.'

'He'll be alright. He's strong.'

I felt May's hand go to the buttons on my shirt. I didn't protest, it seemed a logical way to end the day in the show home. When she had the buttons undone she kissed me from the base of my neck to my stomach. I felt the slow sure pull of desire and drew her face greedily to mine. We kissed hard and long, she held up her arms in surrender. I tugged her dress over her head and pressed her hips to mine. I struggled out of my jeans and we dropped to the floor, thrashing about in the dust. She sat astride me, leaning low and teasing her hair across my face. I caressed her breasts and she arched her back. Then, with another easy movement, I was locked into her velvet warmth. She rocked slowly above me and we made love for what seemed like hours.

We came together and she subsided onto my chest. We slept for a while; I was still inside her. Then the evening chill woke us and she got up and dressed. Neither of us talked about what had happened. There was no need. But our lovemaking had lost its innocence. Before it was unreal, childlike and simplistic. Now there was real passion. Pain, hate, anger and hope: all the requirements of a lasting relationship were within our grasp. But first we had to escape.

'We should go,' I said when we had dressed.

'Anything you say.' Scepticism had crept into her voice.

'You're sure about the address?'

'Of course.'

'I mean, we might have to be there for some time.'

'It doesn't matter. Really. It doesn't.'

The time seemed to be coming when we'd have to talk about the place we were heading to. I suspected that it was the place I'd come from long before, but that recognition no longer hurt. Some sort of change was on the way and it had taken May's madness to bring it to a head. She knew it too, but then she could always see the future more clearly than me. If we'd known the end for us was so close we'd have stayed in the house and talked in the way that both of us needed and neither really could. But there was too much to be said for any start to be made in those snatched moments.

We drove towards the edge of the estate. I didn't use the headlights for fear of the place being watched. By then I was convinced that we were heading towards the meeting I'd tried so hard all my life to avoid. But with May beside me I knew I couldn't avoid it any longer. It seemed inevitable that the address on the envelope was the address of the house with the thin brown room, perhaps of my mother. I tried to picture her face, but I couldn't. As I said, I badgered the home for details about her. Only once did they tell me anything, and I tend to believe it because it came from a Matron who I trusted. I remember I was begging her for a toy lorry in a shop window. She, as always, said that money was not provided for that kind of thing. 'She should buy it for you,' Matron said. 'She has more than enough.' And that was it. She knew she had said too much and my pleas and tears were met with her anger. In the end, to quieten me, she bought me the lorry with money from her own pocket. So, in an indirect way, I always considered it a gift from my mother.

'Cliff.' May's voice cut into my reminiscences.

'What?'

'The envelope is in my bag.'

'Fine. So what?'

'Just in case anything happens and we get separated.'

'I told you, we're not going to get separated.'

'We are.'

A row of lights suddenly blazed into our eyes. What I'd taken to be a low hedge turned into a line of black-coated police. From nowhere a helicopter swooped. A voice crackled through a megaphone. There seemed no way out. Then I felt a rush of air from my left as May opened the door.

'I'm going now.'

'No, May!'

'Listen. Listen to me!' She was full of authority. 'I have an excuse. Remember. They think I'm mad. You don't have any excuses. So go, love. Please go.' She leant over and kissed my cheek. 'I love you, Cliffie. I've always loved you.'

'I love you, May.'

The warmth was suddenly gone from her face. Time seemed to have been suspended. The arc lights glared into the car, the helicopter was directly above. The police were waiting for us to make a move. I kissed May with passion. 'The address,' she pleaded, pushing the envelope into my hands. 'Go now.'

She slammed the door and began walking slowly and deliberately towards the line of police. She had taken one of her plastic bags, but I knew that all that the men would see was her naked body – the massive lights burnt through her thin dress, making it invisible; and she knew it. Then the ranks of black broke and a mass of darkness seemed to swarm towards her. I stood on the accelerator and aimed the car towards the left of the group at what seemed to be a tall wooden fence. Blinded by the lights, I held the wheel straight and the car burst through onto the dual-carriageway. I tore off towards the town with the helicopter nose-down in pursuit.

# TEN

THE HELICOPTER TAILED me to the outskirts of the town. I headed for the tallest building and was soon lost in the tangle of streets. I ditched the car and ran off. It didn't take long to find another vehicle, parked out of the reach of the streetlights in a loading bay behind one of the stores. In less than ten minutes I was away again. When I turned on to the motorway I could see the helicopter in my mirror still hanging over the town, swinging a searchlight beam, looking vainly for a fugitive among the shadows. Two police cars hared past in the opposite direction, sirens blazing, but they were too late. I was gone.

I struck out for London but I could feel the exhaustion behind my eyes. The lights of the motorway blurred and more than once I felt my chin drop as the warmth of sleep beckoned. I knew I had to find somewhere to stop for the night so, at the next exit, I pulled off the motorway and drove through the dark countryside. After passing through a small commuter-belt village, I came to a track with a sign bearing the head of a bull and the name of a farm. I pulled off the road then left the track at the first break in the hedge. I parked the car at the edge of a field, just inside an open gate, locked the doors and fell immediately asleep.

I woke cold and stiff at dawn. The windows were opaque with condensation; a handswipe revealed an empty rutted grassed field which rose slowly towards a copse of trees. The field was bordered by a hedge, beyond it more pasture, and on the slope there was a wooden stable with a horse trough beside it. Overhead the sky was punctuated by a stream of large jets, so I knew I was somewhere in the segment of semi-countryside between Gatwick and Heathrow. I got out of the car and stretched. The air was sweet and already warm. I took off my shoes and socks and padded through the dew towards the stable. When I reached it I plunged my face into the cold, clear water of the horse trough until I could feel the metal base on my forehead. Bursting back out I lay on the ground and watched the clouds that canopied the jets. They seemed lighter and faster than I'd ever known them, as though someone was projecting a speeded-up film of them onto the screen of the sky. There was a pressure in my head which jumbled my thoughts; I closed my eyes to relieve the pain and dropped back to sleep.

When I woke again the sun was higher. I was cold from the water in my hair but felt no hunger, just an emptiness that a cigarette filled for a while. I tried but didn't have a strong enough will to move from where I lay, so I stayed where I was; watching the jets, and fancying shapes in the scudding clouds. For much of that day I remembered nothing about May, or the hospital, or the child. All I knew was that I was lying in a field watching the sky and that seemed to be enough.

I fumbled another cigarette from my packet – the last – and smoked it. Then I repeated the action and smoked it again and again until my mouth was parched and I was forced to plunge my head once more into the trough. But it wasn't enough. The trough had the dimensions of a coffin and with the logic that was dictating my actions I decided to climb in and drown myself. This was not a conscious act of despair, it was just a need that had to be administered to: a hunger that had to be fed. I climbed in and lay face down on the bottom, pressing my arms outwards at each side to prevent myself from coming to the surface. But my body would not let me lie. Its natural buoyancy kept forcing it upwards. So we compromised and I lay face up on the surface of the water, knowing that somebody was shivering uncontrollably but glad that it wasn't me.

I felt for my cigarettes but could not find the packet. Had I done, even though the packet and the matches would inevitably have been saturated and the packet empty, I would have smoked one. Or at least

I would have had the sensation of having smoked one because my mind was now ranging free from its usual moorings and telling my senses pretty much all that they wanted to hear. I suppose I was suffering from hypothermia or something, but after I'd been in the trough for four or five hours – perhaps longer – I was laughing like a lunatic at the peep show of delights paraded before me: I ate everything I wished, I watched the most exquisite bodies pass before me and enjoyed each one I desired, I encountered strange creatures in primary colours which talked in exotic tongues. And I had a long and intense conversation with my mother – which ended as the dream always did – with the journey to the gates of the home.

As the pressure in my head continued to grow, any desire I might have had to get out of the trough receded, and any connection I felt with the figure inside it diminished. So much so that when the sun finally blushed away to dusk the shivering figure in the trough was not me at all. And when I heard the hooves thumping towards me I began to prepare myself to face the devil himself. I felt his foul nasal breath on my face and the texture of his teeth touching mine, his tongue reaching down – huge and swollen, rasping across my unshaven cheeks. But the devil, in this strange negative world, was a horse. In fact it was the horse that lived in the stable and it seemed to want to drink from the trough that I was occupying. So I climbed out and went back across the dark field to the car, turned on the engine and switched the heaters on full so that soon they were roaring hot rubbery air into the closeness of the cabin.

When the fuel ran out after the feverish hours of the night I went back to the stable where, inside, I found a bale of hay for the horse. I hacked it open and tore handfuls away until there was a pile big enough for me to climb into. And there I passed the remains of the night and much of the next day, trapped in a pocket of rancid air. Any movement was uncomfortable because of the cold it allowed in and the shards of hay that were pressed harder against areas of tender exposed flesh.

And that is how the woman found me: a face protruding from a pile of hay showing not the least inclination to offer explanation or regret.

'Hello,' I think I said as she swung the top half of the wooden gate open and stood with a look of amusement and shock on her face. She opened the lower half to allow the rest of the light onto the pile. She was wearing a green jacket, jodhpurs and muddy boots. Her fair hair was tied severely back from the autumn shades of her broad freckled face. Her eyes were wise and wicked. She had a nose, two ears and a mouth but all I ever remember about her are those eyes.

'I know who you are,' she accused.

'Good. Then I won't have to make up any stories.'

She came gingerly into the stable. I suppose she was in her early fifties. The tight jodhpurs accentuated the generousness of her figure but she moved with a casual grace. She was unashamed of her body.

'You kidnapped a child,' she stated.

'Yes, I did.'

'But you gave it back. It was you, wasn't it, who gave it back?'

'It was a mutual decision.'

'You're famous.'

'Good.'

She came further in and stood at the edge of the pile. 'Did somebody put you there?' she asked, enjoying the possibility.

'No . . . I was cold. I needed to come in.'

'Oh, I'm sorry, I wasn't criticising you. I mean it's not every day is it that you, well . . . '

'Will you help me out?' I trusted the woman immediately. By rights she should have been calling for the police but her expression was showing more concern than condemnation.

'Do you want to come out?'

'Yes.' The shivering had begun again. I was feverish, everything in my body ached. I knew I was seriously unwell.

'I don't understand why you took the child and then gave it back. Neither do the press. They're in a tizzy over you, they can't quite decide whether you're an angel or a devil.' She looked at me again, weighing something up in her mind, then she went out, leaving the gates open. After a while I began to wonder if she'd ever been in. Eventually, because she didn't return, I began to reconcile myself to the fact that she hadn't been real.

Then I heard the horse being worked in the field, running in measured strides as only a horse would at the whim of somebody else. And so it went on for hours – or minutes – until she returned with two thermos flasks, a black bucket and a grey blanket.

'I don't know whether it was your fault or not,' she said, depositing the buckets and flasks on the floor. 'I may decide later that it was, I don't know. And if I come to believe that you were responsible for taking the child then I shall have no hesitation in reporting you to the police . . . but I trust my instincts and my instincts tell me I can trust you.' She leant down to pour the water from the flasks into the black bucket and suddenly her face was close to mine and for the first time in what seemed like weeks I smelt the smell of someone else and felt her warmth. She caught me watching her and straightened up quickly.

'You'd better wash yourself down, then we'll see what's to do with you.'

She hesitated before leaving me to wash. I liked her face; the laugh in her eyes made her look much younger than I imagined she was. I sensed possibilities with her and the hesitation strengthened my hunch that the attraction may not have been entirely one-sided.

I washed in the warm water from the flasks and afterwards felt better than I expected. The grime of the past days had been scoured away by the hay and by the shedding of my clothes. They were fit only for incineration. I wound the grey blanket around me; the material was thick and rough and offered some support as I stood. The woman came back in.

'Well,' she observed, keeping her distance, 'so you do have legs. For a moment I thought you'd grown out of the hay.'

'Like a mushroom?'

'Yes,' she laughed. 'It's almost biblical, isn't it?'

'What?'

'You. Shall we go?' She held the gates open for me. The horse had been unsaddled and was nosing at the grass. It looked up, briefly curious, as she led me to her car.

The car, parked just beside the one I had stolen, was new but filthy. The back seat was covered with a blanket similar to the one I was wearing; a pair of wellington boots lay on the front seat; the ashtray was crammed with butt ends all smoked to the same length. The woman took off her riding boots and threw them over into the back before slipping into her driving shoes. Her shoes said as much about her age as anything I'd picked up from our conversation. The engine ignited the radio and that filled the silence effectively enough for neither of us to feel we had to fill it in any other way. Along with having the shakes I was by then feeling nauseous and also immensely hungry. I hadn't eaten or drunk anything bar water from the trough for over twenty-four hours and my body was rebelling at the treatment I had given it.

'I know all about you,' the woman said after we were clear of the village I'd driven through the night before. 'But you don't know anything about me, do you.'

I knew she was only being polite – or what passed for polite behaviour wherever she came from – but I felt I knew quite enough about her to be going on with. The Roedean voice, the muddy jodhpurs, the casual disrespect for her car spoke of someone who had enough money for it to be of little concern. I've never felt comfortable with the wealthy, except for the garage owners, petty hoods and occasional apologetically alcoholic bohemian Barry introduced me to. I suppose I was comfortable with the nouveau riche because I knew I could have made a better fist of it if I'd ever had money. I'd have bought less not more; Barry's service station mate filled his Spanish-style villa with Capo di Monte, he installed a swimming pool and bought lots of gilt mirrors. He was a poor man playing the part of a millionaire and he just looked like somebody who should never have been let out alone with a chequebook. The woman in the car inhabited her wealth. It was as much a part of her as her voice, which meant it dictated her attitudes and that's what intimidated me. We'd never be equal. I could never look down on her. I need to be able to look down on people for any relationship to last.

I suppose it was something to do with the fever, or perhaps I had her marked down as somebody who shouldered part of the blame for May's arrest, but I was suddenly furious with the woman. She was no longer a saviour, just another bundle of needs like Barry. She was trying to play the role of good samaritan when all the time it was me who was helping her out. She needed me more than I needed her. And for what? I dreaded to contemplate the possibilities. Anger came up from somewhere like bile and she caught me looking at her with fury.

'Look. I don't have to help you, you know,' she said icily. 'You can just go back to your pile of hay for all I care.'

'I do know all about you,' I said.

'I see.' She stared loftily at the road ahead and lit a cigarette without looking at it. I took one for myself without being offered it and stole a light from hers. The smoke found its way to my stomach like a flush of warm acid. The woman was trying not to show her irritation, unsure by now of what sort of lunatic she'd saddled herself with. 'You can borrow some clothes . . . And I'll let you have money. But then you can go.'

'Yeah. We'll see.'

'No, I don't think you understand. This is not a bargaining position. This is how it will be.' A thin line of sweat had appeared on her upper lip. She'd just turned through a gateway into a long driveway and I knew she was cursing herself for it. If she'd worked out what was going on a moment sooner she'd have driven on until she'd come to somewhere she could scream for help and have me yanked from the car.

The house showed up after a bend in the drive which seemed to have been tunnelled through a small forest. It turned out to be a largeish thirties mock Tudor effort which should have been much grander following the build-up that the approach had given it. It looked as though it needed some money spending on it. One of the gutters was hanging off, a window was boarded, the gravel drive was sprouting weeds which were also growing at waist height in all of the borders round the edge of the house. It was almost as though the earth was reaching up and trying to reclaim the territory for itself again.

It wasn't hard to picture the inside: the crockery-filled sink, the rumpled bed, the opened drawers spilling clothes, the overflowing ashtrays. It was clearly the house of a well-to-do widow who couldn't cope alone and had seen a chance for a bit of distraction.

I exploded with indignation. 'How can you live like this?'

'What?'

'The place is a fucking mess. Look at it!'

She drew up at the front door, shock cementing her features. I could see that she was telling herself that she'd landed herself with a fully fledged nutter and debating what to do about it. I didn't even recognise myself in what I was saying to her. God knows what I must have looked like: puce with a sky-high temperature, wrapped in a grey blanket and firing off insults like a parade sergeant from the passenger seat of her Ford Escort XR3i. I was using her as target practice for all of my anger and fear and frustration at losing May and walking out on Barry. And I was getting a perverse kick out of tormenting her. 'Get out!' I bullied. 'Let's see inside.'

She hesitated at the wheel, weighing up what few options she had, then she got out without looking at me and fumbled her key into the oak front door. Excited dogs started barking. She calmed them as I followed her in and in that moment I felt pity for her as I felt pity for myself. But her tension had transferred itself to the two Alsatians; they closed ranks behind her and bared their gums as she went into the kitchen and began to fill a kettle.

'Sit down.' She motioned to one of the two cheap fold-up wooden chairs beside a grander dark wood table crumbled with the evidence of a solitary breakfast. The *Daily Telegraph* was spread open at the sports pages. Besides that the room was neat and spruce. There was a single plate and a single bowl in a wooden crockery rack above the sink. The narrow wooden shelf that ran round the room a foot below the ceiling was lined with large jars containing pickled vegetables and more exotic items that resembled mortuary leavings. Jam in rainbow colours was stacked two-high on a pine shelf beside the pantry and a small refinery of bell jars bubbled gas as home-made wines of all hues fermented close to the radiator on the quarry-tiled floor.

It seemed a good enough moment to start again and apologise, but something in her face said she'd already lost whatever trust in me she may have had. Without speaking she put a cup of tea in front of me and fetched an ashtray from the window sill. Then she sat down and we faced each other across the table like lovers after a tiff.

'I don't suppose you'd kill me,' she stated blankly.

'You should know. You know everything about me.'

'You're a strange one.' She moulded her ash on the rim of the ashtray.

'How old are you?' I asked. Something in her interest was unsettling me. She had a way of staring at you that made you feel as though she could see all the way through. I wasn't used to facing that degree of intelligent scrutiny.

She said, 'Old enough to be your mother.' I must have laughed. 'I'm sorry, did I say something funny?'

I had a vision of myself through her eyes and found the view unpleasant. I saw the figure of a fool talking in drunken wisdom to a wiser, sober woman.

'I'm sorry, I need to sleep now.' All of a sudden I felt achingly tired.

'Alright.'

'If you want to call the police, then I wouldn't blame you. But you won't get any trouble from me . . . I promise you.'

'Upstairs,' she said, then led the way through the dark panelled hall and up to the galleried landing. She pushed open the door of a small room which had a desk beneath the window and a single bed. I went in and she followed, pulling down the cover to reveal the starched white heaven of clean sheets. She unwrapped the blanket from me, looked me candidly up and down and gestured for me to get into the bed. I lay down and she pulled the sheets up to my chin. She went over and drew the curtains. Seconds later I was asleep.

# ELEVEN

THE NEXT DAYS are unclear, the edges blurred between consciousness and unconsciousness. When I awoke I was often saturated with sweat, and the breaking back into consciousness was not the normal comfortable easing into the day. I was usually catapulted from my trance state with a jolt, always unsure where I was, always having left some part of my dream world with a terrible sense of regret.

When I came to I craved cigarettes but not food. The woman made me eat. I sipped soup from a bowl which she held to my lips as she supported my head. All of the time, even in the most heated moments of sleep, there was the thrill of the possibility of sex with the woman. I knew she felt the same. Both of us were waiting for the inconvenience of the fever to pass. One day she brought me tablets and a sweet-tasting suspension. The mists began to clear soon after that and after a couple of days of false starts I finally ventured from my sick bed.

The woman was out when I first got up. I drew a bath and looked at my wasted frame in the mirror. I stood on her scales and discovered I'd shed over a stone in weight; my ribs poked through and the flesh on my face was as taut as it had been the first time I'd fetched up at Barry's. I soaked for an hour in the deep tub before wrapping my wrinkled body in one of her bath robes. I then took the opportunity of looking through her cupboards and drawers and laundry basket. In a writing bureau I discovered evidence of a man called Arthur. There was a copy of a will, some bank statements, share certificates and two building society books as well as details of his pension and a life insurance policy. The building society books totalled nearly a hundred thousand pounds, and it seemed from the bank statements the woman was being paid over two thousand pounds a month from his pension. No wonder she owned a horse and was so blasé about her car. It was all very clear: she was bored out of her brains following the death of an older husband. I had a hunch she'd been bored long before.

'Have you seen enough?' The woman walked in to catch me with the details of her financial standing spread around me on her bed.

'How old was he?' It seemed pointless apologising. What I was doing was so out of order the only way I reckoned I could carry it off was by ignoring it.

'You've got a bloody nerve.' She stalked out in a huff, choking back tears of anger. I bundled the papers back into the bureau then discovered an inept testimonial to Arthur written by the chairman of a large merchant bank. It was full of crap about generosity of spirit and how he was an integral part of the bank's success. It went on and on in the same vein. From the letter I was half convinced that the board members had all topped themselves at Arthur's death; it was clear they couldn't have gone on without him. By the end of it he sounded like a closed account. No wonder the woman was bored; he probably was too: the type of man who'd save all of his life for a rainy day only to discover that it didn't start raining until the day of his funeral. I pictured him as a Trevor Howard figure walking through the black and white rain to catch the 6.23 from London Bridge. It would always have been the same train.

Then I found the photo of him and he became real. It showed a lean-faced man with a deep tan. He was fit-looking with a wide smile and he was wearing a green short-sleeved shirt. He had his arm around the woman. They were standing on a small airfield, proudly in front of a two-seater plane. The woman had sunglasses on, her right hand was reaching down to hold onto his, to clamp it to her waist as if she had an idea that she might one day lose him.

I found the woman in the kitchen, cradling a cup of fruit tea. She had been crying, a cigarette burnt away untouched, leaving a long maggot of ash in the ashtray.

'So why don't you tell me about him then?' I offered, half from curiosity, half from sympathy.

'He was passionate . . . he loved life. He really lived his life.' She smiled at the memory of him and that smile told me he was worth a thousand of me. 'They never knew about his passion. Nobody did. Only me. He only ever loved me . . . and sometimes when he smiled – even at the end – and that horrible disease was eating him, you could see the life fighting back. He never lost his dignity . . . we met when he was fifty.'

'And you?'

'I was thirty. I worked for him. I was the clichéd secretary having a fling with the boss.' She caught me watching her sceptically. 'Yes. I worked. All of my life I worked . . . you mustn't make assumptions about me.'

'He was respected. At the bank.'

'You read that did you?'

'Well . . .'

'They didn't understand him. Nobody did. They forced him out. That's what killed him. He needed to have a purpose . . . we should have had children.'

She went to the sink and rinsed her cup. I sensed she was talking as much for her own benefit as mine. When I'd opened her bureau I'd unlocked her past and now she was holding it up to the light to see whether it had faded.

'So why didn't you have kids?'

'We tried for a while. But he didn't really want them. He said . . . he said he was too old to give them the strength they'd need.'

'That sounds sensible.'

She gave me the look again. The look that said I had no right passing judgement on him or her because I'd never truly understand enough about them. Then she unbolted the back door and the dogs followed her into the garden.

I wished I'd met Arthur, he sounded alright. I decided then to stop jumping to any more conclusions about the woman. I suppose it was the house and all of that wealth that did it. I was the one who claimed to need nothing and that was fine while I had someone – Barry and then May – but without either of them I didn't have the cushion of material comforts to fall back on. Still, looking at the woman and her deep-seated sadness, I don't suppose they'd have been a comfort for long.

I think I was mad for a few days. Not barking, just spending too much time in a parallel universe. After the woman had caught me sneaking round the house she'd made it clear she couldn't stand the sight of me so I kept out of her way and spent the time feeling bad about myself. I knew I'd never had many redeeming features but then neither did the majority of the people I usually mixed with. Confronted with the woman's goodness I ended up hating myself. In an effort to avoid my own company I sought refuge with the dogs or in front of the television.

Watching the telly in the day is a factory line experience: long periods of mind-numbing boredom with just enough promise of what's next to stop you switching the thing off. Eventually the act of turning the television off became more daunting than leaving it on so I watched the smiling lobotomised personalities offering pat niceness to half-hearted studio audiences for hour after hour. Sleep was no help because every time I allowed myself to relax I was back in the thin brown room with the looped images of sexual violence. Nothing new was revealed in the repeats, it was just my mind reminding me that if I ever found the house on May's envelope then I might find the room.

One afternoon the woman came into the lounge and sat next to me on the sofa. I was watching a game show and, as had become something of a habit, shouting out the answers to the quiz master. Laura from Basingstoke was on a roll. Two more correct answers and she'd be off to the Canaries with her hubby and four hundred quid in spending money. Despite her crying need for the holiday (her husband had just lost his job in textiles) I wanted her to lose. The woman, of course, took the opposite view and when Laura correctly identified a colour photograph of the prime minister the audience and the woman erupted. The quiz master seemed pleased too. He had his arm round her waist and his tongue down her throat as soon as the answer was out of her mouth. As the credits rolled and the camera pulled back I could see he was whispering into her ear. I felt sorry for the unemployed hubby. Not only had his plight been advertised to the sad nation of daytime telly watchers but his wife was now being groped by a minor celebrity.

The woman flicked the screen off with the remote. The room went cold. I felt her hand go to the top of my neck and my head being pulled towards her. We kissed and then she led me upstairs to her room; it didn't seem to occur to her that we could have continued downstairs. I lay on her bed waiting for her to take the initiative. I'd had little desire since I came out of the fever but the unexpected kiss had awakened something in me and I didn't want to spoil things by pushing her too fast. She lay beside me and stared hard into my face. She was close and we kissed again. She made no protest as I undid her blouse. She held her arms across her breasts. I pushed them aside. I knew I was the first person to see her naked since Arthur's demise. Her skin was old and white but no less beautiful for that. We caressed each other and soon reached the stage where we were far enough away from ourselves and each other for the age of our bodies or the state of our minds not to matter.

We wrestled conventionally, easy in close bucking proximity. She shuddered and stifled a cry as she came; it was a sad and guilty pleasure she found that day. I tried to draw away but she pulled me close into her and then it was all over and we slept, cocooned together beneath the thin top cover of her bed.

We woke frozen in the late afternoon light. The dogs had stationed themselves like gateposts at the end of the bed and sat there uncertainly, having lost their mistress to a stranger for a while. Her name was Mary. Only after that intimacy did I feel I could use her name. I don't ever remember her using mine. She tugged the sheet coyly round her as she padded off to her en suite bathroom. As I watched her go I felt a sudden surge of jealousy for Arthur.

Mary came back after a short while and avoided my eyes. Then she said, 'Was I alright?' and smiled unsurely. I told her she was and that she didn't need me to tell her she was. 'Then perhaps it's not necessary to be alone,' she said and I didn't press her for more. She began fussing with the dogs, which I took as my signal to dress and leave her alone so that the next time we met – downstairs across the table – we'd both be protected again. Somehow the act of dressing was more intimate than that of undressing. I stood in the corridor and watched her without letting her see me. She was a careful dresser and admired the front and back of the completed picture in the mirror before making the bed.

Days went by. We didn't repeat the bedroom episode and it hadn't brought us much closer. We remained strangers in that large house. I fell into the habit of making something to eat at lunchtime and each day at one o'clock we'd meet in the kitchen. She'd talk about the horse or the dogs or something she'd seen in the paper and I listened, chipping in occasionally, with no new experiences of my own to contribute. Neither of us talked about our previous lives; she never pushed me about May and the child and I never quizzed her about Arthur. We lived marking time, easy in each other's company like guests in a quiet hotel passing the winter together.

The papers had lost interest in May's case after making up their minds that she was, indeed, insane. That removed their right to moral outrage although the tabloids did their best for a while on the inside pages. I enjoyed the picture they'd built of me. I was the cynical exploiter of a poor defenceless woman, a violent yob who'd beaten up an innocent cafe owner (little mention of our previous relationship), a vandal who'd smashed up a penny arcade and an animal who'd had the nerve to land one between the legs of one of our brave boys in the NHS. They profiled my brief career as a squaddie and found a couple of blokes in the regiment who were happy to say how unpopular I was and what a bloody coward for leaving them in the lurch when they went off to bully the Argies. One paper even did an item on the company mascot – a donkey – and I was surprised to find that they didn't mark me down for a bit of bestiality too. It became clear that May was not going to have to face charges. She'd carried off the madwoman act to the extent that they'd put her into a secure psychiatric unit under observation and there, I imagined, she'd stay for the forseeable future.

And so it went on for five long weeks: me and Mary living together in a strange parody of domestic life. It was all very civil but it couldn't last. I hadn't been out of the house since I got there and the walls were beginning to close in on me. I knew I couldn't stay there for ever but if I'd remained much longer the relationship would have had to move onto another footing which would have made it much more painful for her when I finally had to leave. It would have been hard for me too, and the realisation of that was something of an eye opener. But the erosion of my sovereignty was well under way by then. May had dented it then run off and left me, and Mary compounded it by caring for a while. But I hadn't forgotten May. Those weeks hadn't taken the edge off the need I had for her, just buried it for a while in some deep cavern.

I woke up one morning and knew I had to go. Mary had brought up a tray of breakfast and suddenly I knew that I'd be in Arthur's monogrammed underpants before long. I toyed with the idea of sneaking away while she was out but decided to do the decent thing and let her wet a few handkerchiefs. In the end it was me who cried and she who did the comforting. Finally we went upstairs and, for a while, held each other on the bed, both needing the contact. Then we went through Arthur's wardrobe so that when I left I carried with me her look of tortured pity along with May's envelope, two hundred pounds in cash and a couple of Arthur's suits in an old suitcase.

# TWELVE

I TRACED THE address May had given me to a house in Maida Vale. It was one of the larger properties on a leafy tree-lined street: Victorian and double-fronted with a pair of bays that protruded into the strip of cracked tarmac that separated the pavement from the front door. The paint was flaking and the windows were curtained with dirty nets. When I knocked, there was no reply so I went back to a cafe I'd passed on my way there to think out my next move.

Later on, the story was the same, which triggered off a panic which soon began to grow. I'd not given any thought to what I'd do if the house on the envelope proved to be deserted. Standing at the unanswered door a second time I decided to give it one more go in the evening, then try to get in by forcing a window round the back. That way, if the house was uninhabited, at least I wouldn't have to find a hostel for the night.

But just as I was leaving, a grey-faced old man in a flapping cardigan appeared round the corner of the next-door house.

'Who you after?' he said, wheezing with the effort of the journey from the back of the house. He stood like a stick man leaning a thin arm on the drainpipe for support.

'Anybody live here?'

'Might do,' the old man said cryptically, fishing for more information to trade against what he knew.

'What: you know somebody who did live here but might not any more. Or you know that somebody did live here but you're not going to tell me?'

The old man rasped in another lungful of air. 'Clever cunt aren't you. What you selling?'

'What?'

'The case. What you selling?'

'Nothing. It's clothes.'

'That's what they all say . . . It's not clothes . . . not dressed like that. You look like a . . . a fucking scarecrow.' I waited, he was straining with another observation. 'Cunt.' It plopped out like a turd.

It was the first time since leaving the army that I'd been confronted with anybody who used obscenities with such pointless regularity. I felt curiously at home with the old man's foul mouth.

'Wogs . . . ' He was off on another vitriolic tack, drawing in more air through blocked airways. 'Moved in a while back. Then the others. Fucking students . . . then the rest. Didn't used to be like that round here.'

'Didn't it?'

'No. Respectable it was.'

'Why did they let you in then?' I'd had enough. I started off up the road.

'You little . . .' he examined the options, ' . . . cunt!' He swung himself off the wall and used the momentum to carry himself towards the back of the house. 'I was going to let you in for a cup of tea but you can just fuck off now.'

'Shame,' I called, backing off up the street. 'I would have liked to meet the missus.'

'Nah. She wouldn't let you in. She's up her bingo.' He waited at the corner of the house for one last opportunity for verbal assault.

'Don't you remember me then?' I knew it was a shot in the dark, but it was worth a try.

'Eh?' He cupped his hand round his ear. His hearing aid began whistling. He fiddled with it and the whistling stopped.

'I said don't you remember me?'

He peered short sightedly as though he was looking at me through a long dark tunnel. 'What you say?' The cogs were beginning to turn.

'It's a few years ago now, dad.' I moved closer to give him a better look but the old fool had misunderstood the familiarity.

'Son?'

'What?'

'Son . . . I don't believe . . . ' I realised too late that the old git had got his wires crossed but he was already lurching towards me like a cripple towards a faith healer: stiff legged, arms held out before him. He was crying bitterly and profusely.

'Look . . . let's get you inside.' I took his arm as he reached me and he pivoted like a child round a lamp post back towards the house. He smelt of washing powder and sweat and seemed to weigh almost nothing at all. But the contact through my sleeve felt sharp, like a claw. He was a fighter.

We cleared up the confusion in the kitchen – another transaction that took me briefly back to Mary, and on the stepping stone of my time with her back to May. By the end of it he was laughing, but not until he'd cried himself dry. He had a lot to cry out. When he laughed so did I but neither of us found the situation particularly funny.

'I can't place you, boy . . . I just can't . . . and I never forget a face. Never forget a face.' He was raking through his memories of old next-door neighbours. 'Of course it was thirty years ago when they turned the place into flats. You can't . . . well, you lose track, don't you. One moment some young girl turns up with her mum and dad and a car-load of plants, next thing a fellow's sniffing around in a sports car. Then she's off with her plants an' a young laddie comes with a noisy record player . . . I don't know . . . the garden's a fucking mess, I do know that. I gave up on the bindweed ten years back . . . Now I can't manage . . . well, Edie has a go with the clippers but it's all she can do to keep the roses pruned.'

He told me that he and his wife had inherited the property on the death of her mother. There had been wealth somewhere down the line but from the poor state of the decoration it was clear that it had run out.

' . . . Wait a minute. I got something now . . . Hold on.' I held on. In his mental game of bagatelle, a steel ball of memories had fluked its way into the nail cradle. 'When would it be, then? How far back did you say?'

'Thirty odd years . . . a woman and a small child. On their own. Possibly not all the time.'

'Nah . . . there was a family. Big family there for a while. They rented the place for a year or so just after it was converted. Lots of kids. They were always rowing in the street, breaking the milk bottles. Edie fell out with her over the kids. He was . . . let's see – Brian, Billy, something like that. Relatives did you say?'

'Yeah. Relatives.'

'Look. See that cupboard over there.' He pointed towards a small oak cupboard in a dark corner of the kitchen. 'There's a bottle of malt. Be a good boy, fetch it here and a couple of glasses, and we'll have another go at it.'

We drank the rest of the afternoon away. Edie never appeared; Ron reckoned she must have gone back to her sister's for tea. He was starving hungry he said but daren't make himself anything in case she hadn't eaten. He was scared to death of her. She kept him locked like a prisoner in that massive old house. He couldn't get out without her and it was clear she didn't much want him to.

I didn't learn anything more about Billy or Brian or whoever it was who used to live next door. It did force me to wonder though. I mean, I'd always thought of myself as a bastard as well as an orphan, but what if that wasn't the case? I knew I wasn't going to get any more answers from Ron, so after we'd polished off the malt and he'd dropped off to sleep in his chair, I took Arthur's suitcase, let myself out of the back door and scrambled over the wall.

The back garden was littered with builders' rubble and glass which crunched underfoot. The back of the house was as unkempt as the front, even in the suburban semi-darkness you could tell that the windows hadn't been painted for years and certainly hadn't been cleaned. A bonfire had once been lit too close to the back wall and the soot silhouette remained along with the residue of damp charred cardboard and rusty tin cans. The whole place gave off an aura of slow decay and encroaching rot.

I broke open a clasp on one of the sash windows but it was painted shut and wouldn't budge. The only other option was to smash a pane and to try and get in without severing an artery. So that's what I did, and got as much glass out of the frame as I could before shoving the suitcase in and following it, head first. Scrambling to my feet, I stood in the centre of an empty room and felt the darkness close in around me.

# THIRTEEN

I LIT A match which spent itself after briefly illuminating a light switch by the door. At the same time I thought I heard somebody moving about upstairs so I froze and tried to work out which room the footsteps were coming from. But when I stopped, the sounds did too, as though whoever was up there was mirroring my movements. I opened the door slowly but the hinges creaked so loudly I might just as well have shouted a greeting up the stairs. The hallway light was switched on which seemed to indicate that the place was not entirely deserted.

The stairs and hallway were better tended than the ground-floor flat. There was a carpet on the floor and the walls looked as though they might have been papered at least once in the century since the place had been built. I knew I should have pushed the man next door for more information; my best guess was that the flat downstairs had been squatted. One of the walls had been painted with luminous fertility symbols – the kind of pagan claptrap that squatters worship. But if they had been in they certainly weren't now: they'd have been on to me like a shot and I'd have been booted out of the front door.

The old house felt like a hospital ward at night: full of sleeping disconnected people. In a hospital, though, you don't sense the brooding threat that sent shivers down my spine as I slowly climbed the stairs. For the first time for as long as I could remember I felt afraid. I've never had a fear of the unknown – you don't have when the only possibilities you have reside there – but I've always had a nose for the more unsavoury kinds of violence. Perhaps it came with the baggage I carried with me through the wrought iron gates of the home. I knew, we all knew in there, which members of the staff to avoid – especially at night. It sickens me more now than it did then. Then I didn't know any better. Now I don't know much worse. But it was Barry who taught me that pain and pleasure don't always have to share the same bed.

At the top of the stairs the light ran out again. I was faced with the doors of three flats leading from the stunted landing. I walked through the middle one and found the flat derelict and vacant. Streetlight flooded into the uncurtained room, an irregularly shaped space, clearly the work of a cowboy converter who hadn't paid any attention to the original layout of the house before erecting his thin plasterboard walls. A few carpet samples had been thrown over the ripped lino that covered parts of the floor. Damp was coming in through the exterior wall, blistering the plaster. In the corner there was a pile of newspapers; they were stained with a dark liquid and seemed to be covering something. I stubbed the top sheets aside with my toe. Underneath two black kittens lay back to back. They were dead but their stomachs were moving, which told of the industry of the dark colony that toiled within them.

Something moved upstairs. It sounded like a heavy chest being dragged across a wooden floor. Then footsteps crossed the ceiling. I knew I had to get out. I reasoned that the place would still be there the next morning and that daylight would make the investigation easier. I decided to climb back over the wall and throw myself on the mercy of Edie and Ron. I went back out to the hallway to find that somebody had switched the light off. At that point, my nerve failed completely. Needing the security of the streetlight I went into the flat next door. It was the mirror image of the one I'd just been into except for a tightly angled staircase which led from the corner of the room to the roof. I caught a whiff of cigarette smoke and a more pungent odour of decay. Another crate was being shifted. Somebody was whistling tunelessly with the effort but they stopped when the stairs creaked under my weight. I heard a door close but carried on up the stairs knowing that if this was to be the end of it then I'd much rather face it sooner than later.

I suppose, deep down, I'd always melodramatically associated the thin brown room with my own death and the higher I climbed through the house, the more convinced I was that I was going to find it. At least it would have been a fitting resting place. Perhaps the house where it had all begun, perhaps not. But it set me wondering whether I'd be discovered like the kittens, twitching beneath a pile of damp newspapers, with an expression on my face of . . . what? Vanity drew me to a halt on the stairs. I had a crazed notion that it suddenly seemed to matter what I was showing on my face when the final blow came. A smile? A look of defiance or anger? But for who? I assumed they'd call Barry in to identify the body. But how was I to know whether or not he'd written me out of his life by then – and if not him then who? I didn't want it to be May. It couldn't be May.

With a huge sense of loneliness I went on up the stairs. I heard a quick laugh – sharp like a shattering glass – then the smell of decay gave way to something sweeter: cheap perfume. I stopped at the closed attic door and listened to the sound of voices from within: men's voices and then a woman, an older woman who seemed to be protesting or pleading but without any real conviction. The men cajoled, the speech of one of them was thick and slurred. There was a slap and then another laugh: rougher, then more pleading, more protestation, a giggle and laboured panting. I pushed the door. It gave a little but it was enough for me to get an angle on the room.

A woman was lying on a long wooden trunk under the skylight. Her dress was up round her waist and her stockinged legs were being held vertical by one of the men positioned at her feet, giving an impression of someone upending a wheelbarrow. This man was watching the woman's face, and in front of him, between the woman's legs, was a younger man: naked; working hard, thrusting his pelvis rapidly and rhythmically as the woman scored weals into his back with her fingernails as she urged him on. Discarded clothes and empty beer bottles littered the floor.

The man inside the woman grunted and slumped. The woman sighed in exasperation. 'Not yet,' she cajoled. 'Not yet.' As he stepped away and before the other man dropped his trousers and climbed into his place I caught sight of the woman's face. It was familiar, even with the distraction of the passion-veiled eyes, the tongue rasping over dry lips, the smeared make-up. It was the face from a long-ago wedding photograph on a dusty mantelpiece. I knew who she was and I felt a surge of pity. But not for her. It was Edie; older, much older than the photos next door. Edie who spent afternoons at the bingo and who had obviously thought better of tea with her sister. I wondered how long this ménage had been going on and whether Ron knew anything about it. I suddenly realised that he probably did and the depth of his bitterness made more sense.

I knew I shouldn't have been watching. But the way the scene was framed by the doorway and lit by the soft orange glow coming down from the skylight distanced it from reality. It was almost like watching something on the telly, softly pornographic and real with the passion of life about it. But it was better than the television. It was dirtier and tear-streaked and the seeds of destruction and decay were already sown into it. Edie needed those men. One man would never have been enough to satisfy Edie, you could see the power of her body and the depth of her passion. She seemed to have an appetite that was beyond satiation. Maybe that was why Ron was clapped out, he'd been knackered by forty years of Edie's demands.

I backed down the stairs. The light had clicked off of its own accord. I felt blindly behind me for a hand rail. Then something came like a charge through the door: a gasp, a cry, the bellowing of a huge wounded animal or the rush of gas through the torn fabric of a crippled airship. Edie had climaxed and the power and shock of it threw me backwards down the steep, narrow stairs.

A thin face appeared immediately in the doorway above. I hadn't registered much about the men in the room but the face was younger than either of the bodies had promised. His fair hair was cut in a wedge and was dark at the temples with sweat, his chest was hairless and thin, freckled and corrugated with ribs. His large penis pendulumed against his thigh, a teardrop of moisture threatening to fall from it. He looked like a working-class walk-on from a late fifties factory film. But he was not angry.

'You alright?'

'Yeah.' I scrambled to my feet.

The other man joined him, dressing hurriedly. 'Christ, I thought it was Ron.' He was older and fatter, in a sharp double-breasted black suit with a bright tie loose at his neck. He had dead eyes. Now he was hopping as he pulled on his slip-on shoes. The sculpture of his dark quiff had collapsed round his temples. 'What do you want?' He elbowed his way in front.

'Message from Ron.' I needed to wrongfoot them.

'What?'

'He wants his tea.'

The older one weighed it up while the other went back into the room to fetch his clothes and to fill Edie in.

'His tea?'

'Yeah. He's starving in there and you're fucking his missus. It's not on, is it?' I started up the stairs towards him, knowing that it leant weight to the lies I was telling him.

'Let me get this straight. Ron wants his tea and he sent you round here to fetch Edie?'

'That's right.'

'Did he mention me?'

'He said to fetch Edie. She's next door. That's what he said.'

'Right . . . right.' He was relieved but I didn't want to let him off the hook.

'Of course he knows. He lives next door doesn't he? How couldn't he know?'

Edie joined him on the landing. She was smoothing her dress: a woman who would have stopped traffic in her day.

'He's lying,' she said with a glint in her eye. She reminded me of a steel-haired Brighton landlady Barry used to know: tall, figure-head proud, corseted. 'What do you want?'

' . . . A drink?'

'You'd better come and join the party then, Cliffie.'

Now it was my turn to play drop jaw.

'Thought so,' she said primly before turning on her heel and going back into the room.

'We'd better be off then, Edie.' There was no embarrassment from the older man. I felt as though I'd broken up a party.

'Lovely, Frank. Lovely.' Edie kissed her palm and blew it towards him. 'Now you look after your dad, Ryan.' She smiled at the other man. He looked embarrassed. His father cuffed him on the cheek. 'Love to Bet then,' she said through a wicked smile.

'Cow.' Frank led the way down the stairs. Ryan followed but looked back up with an offer of something in his eyes.

'See ya.'

'Cheerio, lovey.'

'See ya.' This time to me.

'Ta-ra Ryan.' I mimicked his tone.

The creaking diminished as they went down through the core of the hollow building. I was left looking at Edie.

'So . . . you'd better tell me all about her then hadn't you, Cliffie.'

'Who?' As I came into the attic she handed me a half bottle of Scotch, wiping the neck with her palm.

'May. Who else?'

We stared at each other as I took a pull from the bottle. Ron was going to have to wait a bit longer for his tea.

# FOURTEEN

SOMEHOW MAY HAD got a letter through the censors and sent it to me care of the address on the envelope. Edie had found it on the mat, opened it, and was now dangling the contents, trying to work out what was in it for her. Edie was vicious. She had a core of solid steel that showed in her eyes when she dropped the tart's teasing façade. Having read May's words she'd already sullied them and taken away much of the pleasure I anticipated in hearing from her again.

'So how long has she been your girlfriend then?' She was trying the flirtatious line.

'What's it to you?'

'I'm interested. Just interested.'

'Give me the letter and I'll tell you.'

'She's got a fine hand. She'll not have seen the inside of a factory will that girl.'

'Where is it?'

'It's . . . let me see . . . where did I put it?' She feigned vagueness. I decided to let her play out her hand. There wasn't much point in threatening her even if I'd thought I'd have stood any chance against those bruising arms and sharp nails. 'But of course she's not the only one is she?'

'What do you mean?' I thought she was about to make a play for me so I got up from the chest and, under the cover of lighting a cigarette, moved nearer to the attic door.

'Making demands on you. Wanting you for themselves.'

'I've always been in demand, Edie.'

'Good-looking boy like you. Yes, that doesn't surprise me. Don't think I missed young Ryan giving you the eye.'

'That's a neat arrangement – father and son – keeping it in the family.'

'It suits me.' She dropped her tight smile.

'I could see that.'

'Listen. When you get to my age you take it where you can find it. Alright?'

I couldn't make my mind up whether I liked her or not. I think she was facing the same difficulty, but we were both aware that we were trading on the same market. We skirted a few subjects for a while and then, half a bottle of Scotch later, I realised that she was afraid I was going to shop her to Ron even though she was working hard at not letting it show.

She said, 'Oh yes, I never miss the bingo.'

'And Frank and Ryan. How do they fit in to that then?'

'Well, it's Ron.' She pursed her lips. 'He's not . . . '

But what he was not I didn't particularly want to hear. 'Yes, I've met him,' I cut in.

' . . . interested. Well then.'

'I spent the afternoon with him. Drinking.'

'What – Ron?'

'Yeah.'

'No. Not Ron. He doesn't drink in the afternoon.'

'He did this afternoon.'

'That's not like him.'

It seemed that already I knew more about each of them than either of them knew about each other. Why can't people talk? It's a question that always arises whenever I spend more than a few days in the company of any couple. Perhaps it's because of the fortress of lies – or at least half truths – that people build around each other to keep the relationship together and the rest of the world out. By the end of it you're so far off the ground that the edifice is only visible to someone on the outside. But that doesn't mean it's weak. It'll stand up to any amount of battering because by then your own truths are the only ones that matter and anyone who says otherwise is a liar.

'It's not good for him. Not good for him at all.' Listening to Edie's concern for her old man threw some light on what I felt for Barry. Despite the fact that she was looking for sexual gratification elsewhere, it was clear that she still loved Ron. Companionship is a hard habit to break.

'Are you listening to me?' She could see my attention was drifting.

'Yes. Course I am, Edie.'

'Good. You might learn something.'

'I hope so.'

'You see the thing is . . . ' she wagged a crooked finger at me. 'The thing is, lovey, you think you're a cut above me.'

'No I don't.'

'You do. But we're the same, you and me.'

'I'll give you that. Yeah. There are similarities.'

'Oh . . . similarities. Don't we talk posh.' She tried a haughty look then spoilt it by taking another drink from the bottle. 'No, you see . . . ' She stifled a belch. 'Pardon me. You see, Cliffie – don't mind if I call you Cliffie, do you? – I'm the same. I know I'm a cut above you and you know you're a cut above me. But the thing is: everybody thinks the same. Even Ron does. You wouldn't credit it but he does . . . ' The drink was beginning to hit her hard. 'It must be nice to be young and in love . . . ' Her voice had begun to fascinate me. It was low and shapeless but the cigarettes had begun to give it an edge. It wouldn't be long before she wouldn't make it up the stairs for Frank or Ryan or even the whole bloody British army of the Rhine.

'Look, Edie . . . '

'Yes. I know. You want to see your girlfriend's letter. It's back at the house. We'll go and fetch it. See Ron. Have something to eat. Just give me a minute . . . '

I took the bottle from her and finished it. Edie was trying to compose herself. Every so often her eyebrows went up and her brow furrowed as though she was conducting a silent interior monologue.

'You see . . . no . . . well . . . ' She came at it from another angle. 'I wasn't always unfaithful to him.'

'It's none of my business.'

'No. I'd like to explain . . . '

'Don't want to know.'

'Do you mean that?'

'Yeah.'

'You're a good boy, Cliffie. May's a lucky girl. It is May isn't it?'

'May. Yes.' I wanted to reclaim the word.

'Only her signature was a bit scrawled . . . hurried.'

'I'll read it.'

' . . . I've made you cross now. I'm sorry.'

'Tell me something. Ron said something about a family that lived here. Big family. Barry or Billy or something.'

'Billy Docherty. Irish. Lovely looking man. Lovely skin. He worked on the Underground. He was an engineer, very good with his hands. Tiny little wife. Billy. Yes. Billy Docherty.'

'Children?'

'Oh God yes. Terrible troublemakers the boys. Billy didn't give them the time of day. They ran riot. And he did shifts.'

'What about the girls.'

'Oh, chalk and cheese. His wife used to keep them in line.'

'What about the names?'

'Of the boys?'

'Girls.'

'I remember them all. The three M's they were called – cruel really – Millie, Molly and May . . . Oh!' she said. 'May.'

'Yes,' I said. Bloody May.

She led the way back through the house, balancing carefully on her high heels as if she was walking over a pebbled beach. I collected Arthur's suitcase from the downstairs flat and she slammed the door behind her, checking her pocket for the key.

Outside the night came as a shock of fresh air and I realised I'd been in the house for the best part of two hours. In that time it seemed we'd come to an arrangement: I'd get May's letter, something to eat, a bed for the night, and she'd get my silence. It seemed a fair deal. Only it wasn't a deal. I'd never have shopped her to Ron but that would have been for his sake – not hers. Infidelity becomes betrayal only when both parties acknowledge the crime to each other. As I said, I reckoned Ron already knew about Edie's antics with Frank and Ryan. There was no need to rub his nose in it.

He was still asleep in front of the one-bar electric fire when we got to the kitchen. He was rasping out air through his mouth and drawing it in again through his nose. His face was ruddy and locked tight like a child that has cried itself to sleep. Edie gave him a careful peck on the cheek.

'What time is it?' Ron winced and flexed with the effort of waking.

'I'm sorry, love,' Edie said, showing remarkable control over her state of inebriation. 'I bumped into Cliffie.'

'Who?'

'Cliffie.' She gestured me into the room like a stage compère calling a bottom-of-the-bill act back on stage for an encore.

'Oh. You.'

'Evening, Ron.'

It took him a while to get his bearings. I'd left when he was asleep. Now I was back with his wife who he didn't know I knew from a place he didn't know I'd gone. If we'd have thrown the father and son act into the equation I think he'd have popped his clogs there and then.

Before he could protest at my return Edie said, 'I'll put the kettle on. You sit yourself down, Cliffie. Make yourself at home.'

'Ta.'

'You don't mind if he stays, do you, love?'

'What?'

'Lovely. Pop your coat into the hall. I'll soon have a bedroom aired.'

We had an al fresco meal of biscuits and tinned tongue washed down with weak tea. Edie was still half cut but carried it off by diverting her energies into a stream of manic banter. Ron didn't seem to find anything unusual about the meal and kept his face determinedly fixed on the plate as he clacked with ill-fitting dentures through a pile of Custard Creams and cubes of ox tongue. Neither of us was called on to contribute to Edie's monologue as she rattled through the cast list at the bingo, sketched in some details about the terrible dandruff on the caller's collar and went on at some length about some bitch who'd said something to someone and then sailed off like the Queen Mother. 'Oh yes, and I saw Frankie and Ryan,' she tacked on at the end. 'Lovely boy, Ryan. Said he was looking into soft furnishings. Frank's chest's still keeping him at home. I should think poor Bet's at her wits end with him under her feet all day. But then he's got the Legion hasn't he?'

'Anything else?' Ron, it seemed, was not in the least bit interested in Edie's alibi. I don't think he'd heard a word of it.

'He eats like a horse. You wouldn't credit it, would you. There's nothing of him is there?'

'That's the cancer, Edie, isn't it?' It came out of nowhere. Edie missed half a beat then threw him a strange look of anger and pity. 'I'll open the pilchards shall I?' She was up and over by the sink before Ron had the chance to decline. But now it was Ron's turn. I don't suppose he'd had an audience for his cancer routine before and he used it to keep his wife pinned to the ropes with questions like: 'The consultant. What was his name?' And 'Remission. What did they say about that?' I knew then that I'd fluked into a shared tragedy. I'd thought it was all Ron's, but it belonged to both of them.

Ron had it in the lungs. It was just a matter of time. They'd seen everybody there was to see. It sounded to me as though they'd given up on him early. Hardly surprising when you think of the picture he must have presented to the specialist: seventy plus years old, bitter, poor, no health plan. Why waste expensive drugs on a case like him? In him I saw the ghost of my own future.

Ron's case didn't make me feel angry or afraid. If anything I wanted to laugh. Sometimes at the most inappropriate moments I want to laugh. It's not because I find those situations funny and it's not because the only alternative is tears. It's because sympathy is an unworthy response in the face of tragedy. It denies pride and self esteem, suggests that the onlooker understands something of what the victim is feeling when in truth he doesn't. All we have is the benefit of our own experiences and why should we have the arrogance to believe that they are in some way the same?

But as Ron talked I had a sudden vision of the final morphined moments. Of Edie's silent night-time vigil in the hospice; proud and strong in carefully chosen outfit as Ron queues for the final dose. But before the trolley comes I see him fighting back through the pain one last time and they remember the bench where they first kissed: 'Remember the bench, Edie?' he whispers, and she answers with a tightening of her grip on his hand. Then Edie recalls the first dancehall clinch together: 'The snowball on the ceiling. It was so beautiful.' The silver lights dance across her eyes and she blinks to hold back the tears. Then they both remember the soft rain on the windows of the seafront B&B, where they passed their penurious honeymoon – the season long over.

Then they rush through a cartoon of their lives together for her benefit: to help her remember; to give her something to pass on to the unvisiting son to pass on to his children. But the son does not care for their memories and the gap that Ron leaves in the world is filled as soon as the funeral is over.

I come in on the end of Ron trying to say something to me. ' . . . a churchgoing man?' A question hovers. Is he asking about my faith or questioning his?

I stumble in, 'I'm sorry Ron. I wasn't . . . '

'Yeah . . . well, never mind. Doesn't matter.' I've wounded him and, worse, Edie has gone cold on me. I catch her face in the mirror as she twists back the tin lid of the pilchards. She was thinking that it was the least I could do to listen – the very least.

She strikes back bravely. 'We don't care what we eat now. Do we, Ron? Tinned stuff, cakes, fancies. I give him whatever he wants. Nothing's too good for him now.'

'She spoils me,' he obliges.

'I do not.' The pilchards are borne to the table, head to tail in their shallow bloody grave. They add to the peculiar aroma in the room: Ron's socks and trousers singed by the fire, stale tea, damp walls,

Edie's perfume and cigarettes, a century of cooking smells and dirty washing.

But Edie's manner had definitely changed towards me. She'd sobered up enough to question what a complete stranger was doing at her table. But at the same time it seemed that she still didn't want me to leave. The bargain wasn't complete.

The bedroom was comfortable enough even though it hadn't been decorated since the sixties. Browned and curled newsprint images of cherubic pop stars were sellotaped to the walls. I'd been given the room of the errant son: the nursery where Ron and Edie would once have proudly peeped round the door at the sleeping baby.

I'd declined Edie's grudging offer of an evening in front of the telly. Ron's socks or some peculiar smell emanating from him was beginning to turn my stomach. Anyway, it was hard playing a walk-on part in somebody else's kitchen-sink drama. When I set out for the destination on May's envelope I'd been convinced I was going there for me, to find something for myself. What I found was May's history lurking around that street and I really wasn't interested. But I was hurt. I felt as though a present had been snatched from my grasp after I'd opened it and discovered it to have been something I'd always wanted. The episode made me realise just how right I'd been to shut off the past. Hope is more painful than denial – at least in the short term. As I lay on the bed I made up my mind to close the door for good on the thin brown room. I knew it would take time, but at least the decision was a beginning.

A coal fire warmed the room. I turned off the light, kicked off my shoes and watched the flame shadows dance across the ceiling. Then I remembered the rest of the bargain: May's letter. Edie had deflected any mention of it with promises of 'later' and 'I'll fetch it in a minute'. I put my shoes back on and went to the door. I tried the knob but it was stuck. I pulled harder, it wouldn't budge. It was locked and I suddenly realised why there was a bucket in the corner of the room.

Just as well. The pilchards were working on the ox tongue and custard creams and the churning mixture was being fermented by the whisky which had begun to throw up acid signals to the back of my throat. I vomited copiously and without further warning. I don't think I'd have made it to the bucket even if I'd wanted to.

# FIFTEEN

NEXT MORNING, I woke up to the shock of my life. When the door was unlocked, instead of Edie or Ron standing there, I was confronted by two figures from my past. It was Hollister and, with him, a man called Enright, one of Barry's old clubbing mates. Enright worked in a car body shop spraying paint over the botched-up repairs; he was tall and usually docile but prone to occasional bouts of violence. Hollister hired him on a freelance basis to provide muscle. I'd always got on well with Enright, but the sight of both of them at the door took some adjusting to, especially after the best night's sleep I'd had in ages. I realised why when I woke up: for the first time in as long as I could remember my destiny was entirely in the hands of somebody else.

Hollister didn't wait to be invited but creamed into the room in his camel hair overcoat, stepping carefully over the pile of puke in the corner.

'We also deliver,' I said. Enright sniggered.

'Shut it,' Hollister snapped, and the guillotine dropped on Enright's smile. I realised that things must have changed between them. Enright had always been happy to work for Hollister, he had few scruples and usually went along as much for a laugh as anything. But the tension that now existed between them seemed to suggest that their business relationship had moved on to a much more formal footing. It meant that I certainly couldn't count on Enright's support if things got nasty.

Hollister sat on the edge of the unmade bed, pulling his coat round him to minimise the contact between the expensive cloth and the rumpled sheets. He said, 'You took some finding.' This was a new Hollister – the sequel. Somebody had taken him to bits and refashioned him into a proper gangster. His face looked different too. Then I realised what it was: he was wearing a wig. As he saw that I'd noticed it he winced self-consciously and seemed about to embark on a justification. Instead he patted it to check that the parting hadn't slipped down. But it was a good wig, not one of those shiny numbers that you see on alopecic women – the ones that look as though they've been hoisted from store-front mannequins. 'This is how it is and no interruptions,' Hollister said and his angry stare directed Enright to police the door. He slid across the room sideways like an amateur actor trying to get off stage. But just as he got there, Edie crashed it open with a tray full of tea cups sending Enright sprawling and a fountain of brown liquid scorching onto the carpet. She dropped immediately to her knees and began dabbing at the stain with her apron, then, at carpet level, encountered the vomit. I could have blamed the cat except for the fact that a half-digested custard cream protruded from the mess, indented logo just visible. 'You dirty little bugger!' Edie said as she retreated from the room holding her nose, and leaving the chaos of upturned cups and teapot on the tray.

'Hardly the cunting Savoy is it,' Hollister observed wryly. Even in the closeness of the room his presence and the toxicity of his aftershave had virtually eliminated the smell of the puke. 'See if you can squeeze a cup out of the pot for me,' he said, prompting Enright to busy himself with the tea things. 'Now. Let's get on, shall we? First thing first. Barry is depressed and I don't like seeing my friends depressed.'

'I'm not going back,' I muttered, keen to state my position before we moved further down the agenda.

'Hit him.' It seemed that Hollister hadn't come to bargain. Enright stood up and stepped over with a stupid grin on his face. I thought he was going to pat me on the back – after all we were friends. Instead, he let fly with a right hook to the side of my face. My head started to sing.

'Now where were we?' Hollister softened his tone a little. 'Yes. First thing. Barry wants you back and you're coming back. Second. You're going to pay off the cost of the damage you inflicted on my property.' He went on, explaining in turgid small-town villainese how my little jaunt had pushed him one step closer to bankruptcy and also how Barry had been whining on at him and he couldn't stand being whined at. But underneath it all was the fact that Hollister had his hard man image to protect – also his honorary position as 'The Fixer' – the only man in town who could get you anything you wanted at a price. This time I was the package and the price didn't really bear thinking about. But the prospect of returning to the cafe was so grim that I made up my mind I could take anything Enright wanted to hand out rather than going back to the coast with them. That was until Hollister dropped May back into the equation.

'Yes . . . she's being looked after – privately.'

'What – BUPA?' Unlikely as it seemed I thought for once Hollister might have done the decent thing and coughed up for some health care.

'No – solitary confinement.' A smile flicked over his face. He'd been working that one up in the car, I could tell. Enright sniggered again. By then they were both really beginning to get on my tits. I realised just how far away I'd moved from them since May and I jumped town. I just couldn't go back with them. But I had to find out what he knew about May and asked him whether he'd seen her.

'Yes. Brilliant, Clifford. How else do you think I'd have found this squalid little place?' That answered another nagging question. Hollister must have wheedled the address out of May then slipped Edie a few quid to let him know when I turned up. 'I could make things easier on her you know.' Hollister now stood by the window and was staring out at the bottle bank garden. The morning light was fighting a losing battle against the streaky window, the sky was regulation London grey. Hollister's weight had left a deep impression on the knackered mattress.

'What?' I said.

'How – you mean?'
'If you like.'
'I don't know. Perhaps . . . well, I imagine I could influence the length of her stay in there one way or another.'
'I doubt it.' The prospect of Hollister's influence reaching that far seemed pretty remote, even for such a senior member of the funny handshake brigade.
'Can you afford to doubt it? Or have I underestimated your capabilities in looking after her welfare?'
'Well . . .'
'I mean – perhaps you and she are conducting some brilliantly executed plan in which you get locked into a puke-filled bedroom in Maida Vale while she wastes away in a secure unit for fucking lunatics. I wonder what your next move could be?' He swung round dramatically and the movement made him miss his footing. He stepped into the puke to steady himself, but didn't immediately realise what he'd done. 'Are you going to enlighten me?' he said, then he noticed his shoe. He crossed to the bed and wiped his foot on the bedspread. It should have been comic but it wasn't. If I look back now this is where the final nightmare began. I thought I'd been through it all since I left Brighton but that was nothing compared to what was to come.

If nothing else, before there had always been a way out. When things went wrong there was always the door. But with Hollister by the window drawing Kilroys on the filthy pane and Enright with crossed arms and a severe haircut . . . they had me. My only hope of escape involved keeping May out of the equation, because when it came down to it she was the one standing in front of the door – not those two jokers. But if I'd run out then I don't think I could have lived with myself. More than that, I don't think I could have lived. What little point there was in not laying my neck on a cold railway line or going out in an explosion of drugs or whisky was her. And for the first time in my life I began to acknowledge I had a reason to live beyond myself. I nearly let slip a sentimental tear, it was all so pathetically poignant.

'Yes . . . alright,' I conceded. If there was even the remotest chance of Hollister getting her out then I had to take it – whatever that meant.

'Well that's just fine, Clifford. Just dandy.' Hollister immediately snapped back into his old self. It was the version with the charm and the easy smile, the one that left a silver slug's trail behind it. 'When we met last,' he went on, 'you said, I don't know whether you recall the conversation, you suggested that you'd never taken anything that anybody really wanted.'

'Did I?'

'I've been examining the statement. It strikes me now that one of the reasons for that is that you've never had anything that you really wanted for yourself. Is this a fair assumption?'

It was all too much. The prospect of having to return to Brighton in the company of Abbott and Costello was one thing but the thought of having to listen to Hollister philosophising about my life quite another. 'Look. Can we go?' I said, pushing past Enright. Hollister fell into step behind me.

But before we left, on the way out, I said goodbye to Ron. He was sitting in the same chair in the kitchen. The back door was open, admitting a little of the morning's grey light into the room. Ron shook my hand carefully. There was no sign of Edie. 'Look after yourself,' he said in a tone that suggested what he really meant was 'wrap up well' or 'don't forget to eat your greens', something paternal. Anyway, there was meaning in it.

'It's all bollocks,' he said, and suddenly, without standing, grabbed me round the waist and held on tight.

'Clifford's philosophy in a nutshell if I'm not mistaken,' Hollister said, prising me out of Ron's grasp and propelling me from the room.

# SIXTEEN

ENRIGHT TOOK THE wheel and steered Hollister's black Granada through the tangle of North London backstreets. After an hour or so the tunnel of housing became punctuated by fragments of greenery which eventually joined together, took root and became the countryside. The stench of stale cigarette smoke and orange peel was locked inside the car. Enright refused to open the air vents because of 'pollution' and Hollister wouldn't have the window down because of the draught, so we bickered our way to the coast like overtired backseat children going on holiday.

For a while, Hollister tried entertaining us with philosophical observations about my life and the direction it was taking. When I didn't rise to the bait he gave up and we fell to discussing my current status in the eyes of the law. In their terms I was still pretty hot, and although we agreed it was unlikely that they'd be diverting much manpower to tracking me down, the consensus view seemed to be that I should lie low for a while. Hollister was keen on my growing a beard which, he argued, would add at least superficial camouflage.

When we reached Brighton they let me out at the cafe and watched me from the car as I went in. It was just before lunch and the street was still shrouded in the sea fret that regularly cobwebbed the town, making it feel cold and distinctly unwelcoming. I walked up the back passage and let myself in. Barry must have seen us draw up. He called, 'Is that you?'

'No,' I yelled back. 'It's me.' He came out onto the landing. 'Hello

Barry,' I said to the apparition that had appeared. He looked appalling; ravaged, with dark crescents under his eyes and blotchy skin. His black turtle neck hung loosely on his frame as though he'd shed at least a couple of stone in weight. He caught my look of shock and patted his stomach with a flattened palm.

'Yes,' he acknowledged. 'Come up.'

I went up into the lounge, resisting the inclination to turn into the bedroom and drop Arthur's case off. That would have finalised the arrangement, and I wasn't intending to stay. As soon as I'd found out where May was I was leaving for good. Barry had set out a tray with biscuits and tea on the low table by the old brown patterned 1930s settee. He'd put a paper napkin between each of the piled side plates the way he did when we used to have special guests. The sight of them chimed a distant bell of sadness in my heart. I noticed he'd bought a new deco tea set, but scanning the room I couldn't see any more changes. The picture of us arm-in-arm on the pier like sailors on shore leave was still propped in front of the overmantel mirror, the same orange-backed paperbacks were regimented on the shelves, the tall curtains were immaculately fastened back with their cord ties, the wicker chair was set at its regulation angle by the bay window. Only the smell was different. Having lost the cigarette smoke and orange peel from my nostrils I registered a distant tang of macho aftershave. Smells seemed suddenly to be demanding more of my attention, something I puzzled while Barry waited for me to say something momentous. I ended up wondering whether I might be going blind and my sense of smell was becoming more acute to plug the gap. Then I realised that over the past few days I'd virtually stopped smoking and maybe that accounted for it. It's strange where your mind can take you when you don't want to be where your fate deposits you.

'Are you back then?' He'd given up waiting for me to begin and started eagerly pouring the tea. His hands were shaking so much that the spoon was vibrating in the saucer. I could see his forehead had broken into sweat.

'Careful, Barry, you'll spill it.'

With a great force of effort he managed to put the cup back onto the table, then he used both hands to hold the teapot as he poured it out.

'New tea set then?' I said, for the want of something to say.

'Yes. I got it at the Gardner Street market. Ten pounds. Not bad was it?' He looked at me with a familiar plea for approval – as if I was the only one who could give whatever it was he'd bought the value he wanted it to have.

'You got a bargain.'

'I thought . . . yes, I know.' He looked boyishly happy.

'Thanks.' I took the cup from him, sipped the tea and immediately had the urge to smoke a dozen cigarettes one after the other just for something to do, just to have an element of control over something.

'So are you back then?' He tried again.

'For now.'

'I'm glad, Cliffie. I'm so glad.' He put his hand on mine in an attempt to break through the strained formality between us. I pushed it away.

'I didn't come by choice you know.'

'I know.' He stared at his shoes.

'But you made me.'

'Yes.'

'Against my will. You made me come back here against my will . . . you sent that thug after me. Barry, I can't go back . . . you said you knew everything about me.' Why I was trying to convince him I don't know. Perhaps I was trying out the line for my benefit.

He said, 'I love you.'

'Oh Christ!' I jumped off the settee and sentried up and down the room. Barry watched from the comfort of the settee. But we were playing out a scene together that belonged to me and May. 'Look, Barry, we have to talk.'

'Yes. Of course,' he said eagerly.

'Properly. Talk properly. We need to get a few things straight.'

'Anything you say.' He'd glimpsed a ray of hope somewhere in the offer.

'Are you taking something?' I suddenly noticed that his pupils were like black beads.

'Anti-depressants.'

'I thought so.'

'They help me get out of bed in the morning.'

'Yes you were never . . . Oh God! Why can't I talk to you!'

'I thought that's what we were doing.'

'Why? Why can't we be straight with each other?'

'I'm not sure I'd like that.'

'Oh grow up, Barry!' The cafe bell went. 'A customer,' I said as the old reflex kicked in.

'It's alright. I've got somebody in.'

'Really?'

'A boy. He's called Charlie. It's not what you think.'

'I don't think anything. That's what I'm trying to tell you. I don't care what you do. I don't want to be here any more. Don't you understand!'

'I thought I meant something to you.' He stirred some skimmed milk into his cup of Earl Grey. I thought my head was going to explode. Something seemed to be filling all the cavities and pressing outwards. I knew I had to get out of the room. Barry got up to follow. I snapped at him to leave me alone and went downstairs.

The new boy was behind the counter. From the look he gave me I knew Barry had been lying when he said that there was nothing between them.

'You must be Cliffie then.' His voice was half an octave too high. It wavered uncertainly around the note as though somebody had kicked him hard in the bollocks. His pretty docile face was familiar but unimportant. He was a figure from the fringes of our life together; one of the well-dressed youngsters that turned tricks for the conference trade to finance a designer label habit. I took a Coke without asking and carried it over to an empty seat by the window. Then I saw a familiar face, the old bloke with the dead wife, so I went to sit with him.

'It's better than a soap opera, this is,' he said without preamble. 'Just when we thought you were gone for good you come back – but now your mate's got a new nancy boy in.'

‘I met your brother.’ I offered him a cigarette. He took one without thanks and lit it without sharing the light.

‘I haven’t got a brother.’

‘Yes you have. His name’s Ron. He lives in Maida Vale.’

‘Oh yes, I forgot, you’re gone in the head as well as queer.’

‘How’ve you been keeping then?’

‘Mustn’t grumble.’

‘Why break the habit of a lifetime?’

‘Well, if you really want to know, your mate put the prices up last month so I started going to the place on the bus station. Then they did the same so I came back here.’

‘I’m sure Barry breathed a sigh of relief. I mean, if he’d lost your forty pence a day he could well have gone under.’

‘So where’ve you been?’

‘I don’t know. Away.’ His interest in my life caught me by surprise. He was one of those people you felt comfortable with solely because you knew they weren’t remotely interested in anybody but themselves.

‘Where?’

‘Why do you want to know?’

‘Why not? I’ve got fifteen minutes to kill before my bus.’ His look was a challenge to entertain him.

‘I went . . . I met a woman.’

‘A woman?’

‘It does happen you know. Anyway, I thought I’d found . . . oh I don’t know what I found.’

‘Go on . . . ’

‘I thought I’d found something I didn’t have before.’ I realised I was still trying to make sense of it myself.

’And did you?’

‘Did I?’ I don’t know. Did I? . . . It was hard to acknowledge, or even to begin to acknowledge, but seeing Barry again, just being with him . . . I don’t know, there was something I got from him I knew I’d never find anywhere else. Something unconditional. You can’t buy that kind of love.

‘You’re a bloody mess, aren’t you?’ Somewhere in his observation was an offer of sympathy. But he was the one who'd gone to seed. He stank like a tramp and the collar of his mac shone a silverfish grey. '. . . Anyway,' he pushed on, catching me looking at him, 'I thought the police were after you.'

'Have they been here?'

'Not as far as I know.' He leaned forward and dropped his voice. 'Do me a favour.'

'What?'

'Get your mate to do something about the tea. It tastes like piss.' He drained his cup of the last of its dregs. 'You look terrible. Bloody terrible.'

'Do I? Thanks a lot.'

'I'm surprised he wants you back. I really am.' To reinforce the point he glanced over at the new boy behind the counter who was watching us with curiosity.

'Oh oh – look out!' The old man caught sight of his bus taking on passengers at the stop at the bottom of the hill. 'Number seven. It must be the half past running late.' He buttoned his coat. 'Don't forget about the tea.'

As he made to go I realised that for all of his faults he was one of the few cafe regulars I felt I could really trust. I called after him, 'Do I stay or do I go?'

'You want my advice?' He was both flattered and surprised.

'Yes.'

'Get out of here. Go as far and as fast as you can.'

'Why?'

In reply he looked again towards the boy then walked out of the cafe. He left the door wide open and crossed the narrow street. I saw him climb with difficulty up the short step of the bus then fumble for his pass. The driver set off before he could get to a seat. A young woman stood and supported him to the back of the bus. With his guard dropped he looked old and lonely and frightened.

The bus passed out of sight of the window and the boy came over, a tea towel draped over his arm like a wine waiter. He said, 'You don't remember me do you?'

'What?'

'Where we met?'

'No. I don't.' I didn't care either. The last thing I needed was to get entangled in Barry's current relationship.

'You smacked me round once.'

'Give me a clue.'

'Twenty questions is it? . . . It was a pub. You were giving me the eye. I followed you into the bogs. You were horrible to me.'

'Oh you. You got me on a bad day.'

'And Barry?'

'What?'

'He got you on a bad day too, did he?'

'That's between me and Barry. Now piss off, you're beginning to annoy me.' He'd been kicked many times. You could tell by the way he didn't even break his stride.

'I looked after him.'

'So what?'

'So . . . ' For a split second he was unsure of himself. 'So don't spoil it.'

'Look. I'm not here by choice. And I'm sorry about your face but you probably deserved it.'

'Got any cigarettes?' He slid eagerly into the old man's seat with exaggerated campness. It wasn't a part of him, it was an act he could put on at will. As I said, there were any number of them round the town – every look was an invitation.

I passed him a cigarette; he took it as a permission to press his point. 'Perhaps it would work out.'

'What?'

'I wouldn't mind sharing. I could kip in mad May's room.' I must have caught my breath or something. ' . . . It's alright, we cleared it out. There's plenty of room.'

'You had no right.' What I was beginning to feel for the boy went beyond anger. I felt in my pocket for some keys, a blade, something sharp and hard I could score across his stupid face to finish the job I'd started the last time we met.

'Barry said it was alright. It was full of dolls and bundles of old letters, boxes of photos. It was all tat, she had terrible taste.'

'And what did you do with it?'

'We took it to the tip. Barry borrowed a car.'

'I see.'

'See – it could work out.'

My anger had swiftly translated itself into a kind of numbness. I don't think my mind could take any more emotional swings. I'd used up my repertoire on Edie, Ron, Hollister and Barry.

I knew that May wouldn't have wanted to return to the cafe, but that wasn't the point. It was as though they were all trying to destroy her, to eradicate any last traces of her so that they could pretend she never existed. I went upstairs and challenged Barry with it. I ranted for a while about how mean-spirited he was – about how pathetic a gesture it had been to throw all of her possessions away. He took all I threw at him, stony faced, as if he was glad he'd provoked a reaction in me of something beyond sheer indifference.

Then, when I ran out of steam, he said in his most forgiving voice, 'Oh Cliffie, you're so . . . how can you expect other people to live by whatever codes you decide are right when you live your life exactly how you want?'

'I don't know what you mean.' He pursed his lips a couple of times but didn't take the bait. Instead he tried to pick up on the earlier conversation, only this time on his terms. He seemed to sense that the longer I stayed the more control he was going to have over me. But something didn't ring true. Even as he talked I sensed that he knew the battle was over and he was saying all the things he wanted to say because he knew it was his last opportunity.

'Should I ask where you've been?'

'If you like. That might be a start.' I sat down on the wicker chair to re-open the negotiations.

'I still have the right, do I?' Barry hunched up to the end of the settee to get as close to me as he could.

'Don't push it, Barry. I went away and came back. "A return ticket," I said to the man at the station. "Where to?" he asked. "Here, of course," I replied.' I was surprised at how quickly Barry's anger came. Before he'd always been a brooder, anger always a last resort – after the tears and always controlled. Not any more.

'Look! I'm not the one who walked out. I've not changed. I care. I'll always care. So there's no need to take it out on me because you're so bloody miserable.' He'd gone puce. He stood up and made to come towards me, then stopped as if he couldn't quite decide what it was he wanted to do. Then he started re-arranging the ornaments on the mantelpiece. I think, in the muddle of my return, he'd forgotten the etiquette of our rows. Usually we took up positions in distant seats and hurled abuse across the room. Perhaps he was more physical with the boy.

'I'm not miserable by nature. You just bring out the worst in me,' I egged him on.

'Thanks, Cliffie. Thanks a lot. Anyway, it's not me – it's her. You've not been the same since she first flounced into the cafe, so don't lay it all at my door.'

'If it hadn't been her it would have been somebody else.'

'Untrue. That is patently untrue and you know it.'

'Okay, so it's her. What can I do? What do you expect me to do about it?'

'Hurt. I expect you to ache and hurt and feel like shit each time she's not there when you wake. I expect you to lose your appetite and watch every dawn and come out in boils and not to be able to get drunk no matter how hard you try. That's what I expect you to do because that's all I can do.'

'You're talking about obsession, not love.'

'What's the difference? What's the difference!' He'd started shaking like an hysterical child trying to make itself sick. He was also on the way to his tried and tested nutter's routine: hands in pockets, staring eyes. I guided him back to the settee, took his hand and the shaking began to subside.

'Where is she now, anyway?' he finally said, chewing hard on his left knuckle.

'I don't know. Some secure psychiatric place according to Hollister.'

'No. I mean where is she now?'

'That's where she is. I just told you.'

'Oh.'

'What do you mean – Oh?'

'Hollister didn't tell you then.'

'What?' I had to stop myself from grabbing him by the collar and shaking him.

'She's out.'

An invisible mule walked into the room and kicked me in the stomach. 'When?'

'Sometime. Last week. I don't know.'

'Out.' Everything suddenly changed. May's release allowed my release. Hollister had lied to get me back to Brighton, but there was nothing now to keep me there. I supposed that he thought once I met up with Barry again then everything would be alright and we'd make it up. But I was off the mark. His reason for bringing me back was much more sinister, and much more in character.

'She's still in a hospital. I mean she's out of the secure place,' Barry continued jealously.

'I thought it would be years.'

'She wasn't charged, was she. Typical of her to get away with it. It was a back door act of mercy thingummy – all that jargon. They didn't even defer a sentence.'

'So she's clean.'

'Yes. Clean. Sane. That's a joke, isn't it, Cliffie?' He tested my appetite for betrayal.

'She's the sanest person I know.'

'Really?'

'It's only the truly sane that go mad in this world. Because they're the only ones who truly see it for what it is.'

'And what's that?' he said bitterly.

'A long bloody chasm of pain from start to finish. There's no solution to it – only madness or drink or suicide.'

'A simple but telling philosophy.' This was from Hollister who'd come up the back stairs and slid into the room without either of us noticing. His arrival sparked surprise in Barry's face and I suddenly began to feel uneasy..Hollister was fast becoming my least favourite person. I dropped Barry's hand and moved back to the window, wanting to put as much distance between me and Hollister as I could.

'What has she done to you?' Barry asked.

'Oh, she filled in a few gaps. Taught me a few things about myself.'

'A clear case of the blind leading the blind I'd say,' Hollister chimed in. 'Anything you'd care to share?' For some reason he didn't have his wig on.

'Follow your whims, Mr Hollister. She taught me that. And that love can heal.' I turned my back on them both them and offered these thoughts through the bay windows and towards the sea.

'Childish crap,' Barry spat.

'What's wrong with childish sentiments? I'm tired of being grown up. I've decided it doesn't suit me.' I sat in the wicker chair but then, intimidated by Hollister standing by the door, jumped straight up and continued Barry's re-arrangement of the mantelpiece knick-knacks. I kept them both in view in the overmantel mirror.

Barry said, 'I don't think you ever did grow up, did you, Cliffie? Anyway, unlike May, some of us choose to grow.'

'It's not a matter of choice. It's entirely out of our hands. We grow up. Then we die – whether we like it or not.'

'I think what friend Barry was trying to say . . . ' Hollister said, trying to chip one in from the corner flag. But Barry intercepted it, 'Well either way, let's not deceive ourselves. Somebody has to pay the mortgage on Never Never land. May'll never make the repayments.'

'Life's one big profit and loss account to you, Barry, isn't it? I pity you sometimes.' It was a cruel jibe, and an inaccurate one. Barry would have given anything to anybody who needed it. He was the most selfless person I'd ever met, but the row, as always, had passed into that phase where baseless abuse was called for.

Then Hollister stopped it dead. 'Save your pity for yourself. You're going to need it.' And the look with which he delivered the warning flashed like traffic lights from good humour to pity to cold anger.

I saw that Hollister had now stationed himself by the living room door like a back-street bouncer. An idea was beginning to form in my head but it was too horrible to contemplate. It was something along the lines of betrayal and revenge. I knew I had to get out of there and fast.

'I need the bog,' I said. 'Too much tea.' I launched myself across the room and collided with Hollister but he stood fast. I swung round at Barry. 'Are you expecting guests?'

'No. I'm not expecting anybody.' We'd picked up the danger signs at the same time. He got up from the settee and went to the window to look. Almost immediately I heard footsteps on the stairs: heavy, booted, steel-toed, three or four pairs. Hollister opened the door with a flourish and a sea of donkey jackets flooded in. The room was suddenly full of the stench of stale sweat and the smell of concrete and tarmac. There were three of them – squat, broad, sinewy labourers, built like postboxes, with windburnt faces and a surfeit of tattoos.

'So this is why I'm back is it?' Words fail you in moments of real terror.

'Time to settle a few scores, Clifford,' Hollister said like a quiz show host. 'I don't imagine we'll meet again. At least for some considerable time. But should you miss the significance of the occasion, this is where you make the final payment on your account.'

'Tasty. Real finesse, Hollister. And these are all fellow masons are they?' My mouth was dry but I think I was still carrying off some semblance of normality.

'I feared Enright wouldn't be up to this one. If you want a job doing properly, go to the professionals. Mm?'

One of the donkeys started filleting his nails with a Stanley knife. I embarked on my final option: pleading to Barry's better nature. 'Barry . . . ' He was back in his wicker chair – the one place in the world where he felt safe – and he was refusing to look me in the eye. 'Barry?' Finally he had to look up.

'I swear I didn't know.' His eyes had swollen with tears. He was hugging his arms to his chest.

'Oh pull yourself together!' Hollister snapped. My last hope was gone. By then I was praying that they'd been given instructions to finish it rather than simply to do a carve-up. I'd rather be dead than have my looks stolen from me.

I picked up my jacket and slung it over my shoulder. I had a sudden vision of Frank Sinatra on an album cover. 'Shall we go?' I said to the donkeys and led the way out of the room. I knew it wouldn't happen there: Hollister would have lined up a warehouse, or at least a venue far out of earshot of a residential area. I found myself wondering if they'd been instructed to take my lips off with the Stanley. It was a form of punishment pioneered in the Province and now beginning to find favour with some of the more adventurous villains on the south coast. I tried to control the churning in my stomach. Being cut deep with a cold blade was one thing but giving Hollister the satisfaction of knowing that I screamed through it all was quite another.

# SEVENTEEN

All I recall about the next few hours is being bundled into the back of a Transit van and driven fast through Kemptown and up the hill to the racecourse. When we got there I was pulled out and marched across a car park to the grandstand. One of the donkeys wrenched a padlock from a door with a crowbar and then we were in the well of damp darkness beneath the tiered stand. I waited for it to happen but it didn't happen straight away. There was a calculated cruelty in the way they took off their jackets and piled them up, then rolled up their sleeves to reveal ham-sized forearms. One of them felt for his knife in his pocket. Then they walked slowly towards me.

When I came round I was in the car park of a large supermarket. It was night – it could have been a few hours after the attack or a day later. I could see a boy parking a long train of trolleys, shunting them rat-a-tat-tat against each other. He controlled the swaying skilfully from behind. All the time I watched him I was aware of the pain – the sharp razor pain. He weaved round in the floodlights collecting more and more trolleys. The lights were huge; tall and towering like something out of Alice in Wonderland, each a cluster of four dropped pearls of white anchored at the base by four sturdy steel bolts. Only the heads of the bolts showed, the shafts had been plunged deep into the ground.

I was aware of a pain more intense than anything I had experienced before but forced myself to focus on other things. Like the boy. The boy with his spectacles that caught the lights, his rolled-up sleeves and stub of pencil protruding from his top pocket (a pencil or pen? He was just too far away to see). I seemed to have been put/thrown/dropped into something behind an orange yellow plastic container marked 'GRIT'; a huge child's toy with a broken lid and the grit beginning to spill from the front. That was why the boy was unable to see me. I was in the monochrome shadows. I couldn't feel my face but I knew that I was crying, I could taste the salt on my . . . I knew where I was. None of that shit about 'Where am I?' – none of that B-movie stuff.

But it must have been late because the huge car park was empty bar a few scattered cars and one burnt-out wreck by the white bit of cliff that the car park had been gouged from. He was making it snake now; the line of trolleys was snaking like a wave as he twisted them left and right, throwing a long heavy motion through the goods train. The boy was young – he was closer now – sixteen, seventeen, a high school kid on an evening job – or perhaps he was simple and it was the only job he could get – but by Christ he could move those trolleys in that hot night. Or perhaps it was cold. Yes, it must have been cold because I could see my breath. See it. See the boy. My eyes were fine but my body wasn't.

Now there was another boy. He called out in an adolescent whine ' . . . Bensons . . . ' – the gold flash of a cigarette pack proffered between them. Then two white tubes lit from a plastic lighter as they both leaned on the train to smoke, taking the moment for themselves, making the most of the warmth of the evening and the promise of everything that lay before them. They were heroes and they both knew it. The world waited for them to pronounce how it would be once they took it for themselves. To them, that evening, the world waited.

And I waited. I waited because I knew that I was dying and my life lay in their hands. I couldn't move. I was not tied but I could not move nor could I crawl or call. Oh yes, Hollister knew his professionals, you had to respect him for it, he knew a hard man when he saw one. Even those three lumps of muscle and cartilage.

The boys finish their cigarettes. They flick them into the night and they die like tiny meteorites in an arc of sparks. Their shift is coming to an end. The apron of the car park has been scoured of its carriages. They each take an end of the train. A laugh breaks and bounces across the warm cold tight night to me. I hold it in my mind like an acid dream until it dies.

I ask: May where are you now?

But why do I ask? I know where you are. You are in a warm world. In a lounge thick with acrid cigarette smoke watching the telly with your fellow inmates. You talk to them but you are not the same. You will never be the same because you understand them in a way that they will never understand you. We understand each other. Yes. That is what ties us together. We know enough to know that we know almost nothing. But you have a blue Senior Service ashtray. The woman beside you is flicking her ash into the polystyrene cup she has just drained of its last gritty contents and you laugh together. Perhaps you are talking about me. But you are still sedated. The last months have made their mark on you. They have screwed the lid on tight with their chemical coshes and sometimes you wonder if I am real.

Am I real?

Not for much longer.

But wait. The train is now coming my way. The boy at the front; the better-looking one, the one with the Bensons and freshly laundered white shirt and blue tie under his supermarket jacket, has seen another trolley, perhaps the last trolley, and now I see it too. Now I am aware of it because I now know that the silver trellis at its base is making marks on my spine. But he cannot know that. Not yet, because he is showing neither fear nor excitement. All that he can see is the end of it, sticking out from behind the GRIT container with something in it. From a distance it must look like a black plastic rubbish sack. But it is not a sack. Nor is it black. The shadows I lie among have rendered my suit devoid of colour.

But then the boy sees something. He tugs at the sleeve of his mate and his mate sees it too. It is me. The prettier one makes a steady slack-jawed approach, the trolley jockey behind ceases his joshing and they bunch together, children again, shoulder-to-shoulder in solidarity. They continue their Siamese approach, drag-footed now in horror at me.

Me.

But I am still far enough away for the shadows to obscure who I am. What I am. As far as they are concerned I could be inanimate. But some signal tells them I am not.

Then suddenly they stop and I fear they are about to run. With a great force of effort I raise my head to indicate that I am still alive. Barely, but still alive. And the pretty one screams. And now the other one vomits. He supports himself with his outstretched arm on the shoulder of his friend. I need their help and they know it but they are helpless. And I know that I am no longer desirable. And I curse myself that, despite my promise to myself, it will have been reported to Hollister that I screamed and I screamed.

# EIGHTEEN

SOMEBODY WAS PUSHING a trolley past me when I woke. I was lying in a suffocatingly hot, white-lit room, insulated by four bare walls from the ward next door and the rest of life going on all around me. I felt like shit. My head was tender to the touch. It felt twice its size. I was tethered to the bed by a drip and a wire which was monitoring something vital. My chest and right leg were swathed in bandages which were regularly changed by a succession of smiling, sometimes sullen, angels. Without exception they winced at the carnage beneath the coverings. I couldn't bear to look but eventually I did and when I did I wished I hadn't. I couldn't crap either, the painkillers had bound me up tight. I craved a decent bowel movement and a cigarette.

To add to my misery there was also somebody keeping guard at the end of the bed: a succession of coppers, rarely smiling, usually sullen. The older ones called me 'Sonny Jim' and spent much of the day in the canteen or in the bogs having a crafty fag. They tried to flirt with the nurses but few were prepared to play the game. The younger coppers in their well-pressed uniforms were more eager and came in on shift changes tense and alert as though they were minding a master criminal. Within a few hours they were usually relaxed enough to be conned into running errands.

Daily I totted up the cost to the taxpayer of my minders but it gave me no joy. I was under arrest and knew that soon the cost of a long stay in prison would be added to the bottom of the bill. I didn't care much. I didn't care much about anything. My free will had been surgically removed when they stitched me up. For the next few years I knew that I would be living entirely without choices. The prospect was frightening, especially as it removed the possibility of a reconciliation with May. But besides my fear of losing touch with her I wasn't angry any more. I was even feeling more charitable towards Hollister because despite the bruising and the carve-up, his donkeys had obviously been instructed not to touch my face. The filleting went on downstairs and hurt like buggery but so what – I was still alive. So what?

After a month in there I was going mad with boredom. I craved a visitor but none ever came. I couldn't even see the telly so my view of the changing world was limited to the conveyor belt of activity that passed my door. I hadn't heard from May and even Barry hadn't been in touch. I didn't want to see him, but it would have been nice to have refused his offer of a visit. So I lay there stewing in my own juices. I couldn't even be bothered to read. There was a pile of two-inch-thick paperbacks on the bedside cabinet, but the blurbs on the back were enough to put me off all of them. I longed for something that had some bearing on my own life, but the nearest I came to it was the daily litany of horror in the tabloids.

My boredom was relieved by the bandage changes. They went like this: A new nurse would come into the room bristling with Wren-like efficiency. This would set off the copper's crumpet radar and he'd sit up a little straighter in his chair. Then he'd bend over in the pretence of doing up his shoelace as she bent over me. Once he'd seen what he wanted to see beneath her skirt he'd usually catch me watching him and wink. At this point I'd register disdain, too busy offering up my scars like favourite children to the nurse.

'So what happened?' the latest one asks.

'Fell downstairs.'

'I only asked,' she says, hurt. I forget that she, like all nurses, is entirely good and innocent, while he, like all policemen, is entirely bad and guilty. 'I only asked,' she says again, this time to elicit the sympathy of the copper. He is one of the rookies with polished shoes and a polished hairless face. He is stumped for a reply but says, 'Knifed.'

'So that's what it was.' The nurse masks a smile. She is even younger than the copper but is way ahead in the maturity stakes. The copper coughs to hide his blunder.

'It's healing nicely,' she says and peers for a while. A faint smell of antiseptic and mincemeat escapes from beneath the sheets. I have an urge to break wind to relieve the appalling pressure in my stomach but feel that this is not the time.

'If it's healing, why does it hurt so much?' I ask.

'Because it's getting better.'

'Ah. Right.'

She straightens the sheet and tucks me up tight, finally plumping up my pillows. I feel cared for.

'Fancy a drink sometime?' The copper makes his play. A less appealing prospect I cannot imagine so I intercept his offer. 'Lovely,' I say. 'We could make an evening of it. Take in a movie or something.'

'Not you,' he barks. I wouldn't have thought he had it in him. But the girl has picked up on something and it's obvious that she's interested.

'What about my boyfriend?'

'Don't know,' says the boy policeman quick as a flash.

'I'll think about it.'

'You do that, love.' He smiles coldly. I can already see him in his pipe and slippers discussing his new lawn strimmer with the next-door neighbour. People like him don't deserve respect. They don't even deserve to be given the time of day. Most of them haven't been – they end up as coppers so that people are forced to take notice of them.

'Don't do it,' I say.

'Dangerous is he?' the nurse asks the copper. But already I'm invisible to them. It's too late. Contact has been made.

'Him? No. Quiet as a mouse.' He grows in her estimation. I say nothing. Then I throw caution to the wind and fart loud and long. The room quickly clears and I enjoy some rare solitude.

A couple of days later I was snatching some sleep while the prescribed pain killers were holding the hell at bay when I was woken by a cough. Immediately I registered a familiar smell: unwashed mac and old newspapers. I opened my eyes.

'Told you. I bloody warned you about this.' It was the old bloke from the cafe. I was so glad to see him I could have cried.

'Yes,' I conceded. 'You warned me. I remember.' I sat higher on my hard pillows. I didn't try for sympathy, but he saw the pain on my face which the movement had provoked.

'They shouldn't though. They shouldn't have done it like that.'

'Show you my scars if you want,' I said gamely, wanting him to know that as far as I was concerned I was alright. He was leaning forward in a borrowed chair by my left side, the perpetual spectator, on his lap a crumpled brown bag of grapes.

'Are those for me?'

'Yeah. Seedless.'

'Ta.' I took the bag, snapped a solitary grape from the tiny bough then said, 'Help yourself.' He took the bag and put it back on his lap. Honour was satisfied.

'I read about it in the *Argus*,' he volunteered.

'It made the *Argus* did it?'

'Unknown assailants. Why didn't you tell them who it was?'

'What's the point? I had it coming. They were just doing their job.'

He raised an eyebrow. 'Very understanding I'm sure.'

'Is that today's?' I gestured towards a newspaper protruding from his pocket.

'No.'

I waited for him to offer it but he didn't. 'So. Tell me some good news.'

'Your mate's still got the new nancy boy in.'

'Yeah?'

'Doesn't say hello any more – Barry – doesn't say much at all now really. He looks terrible.'

'Really?'

'Terrible. They're always fighting. The tea's still poor but it's improving.'

'Anyway, how did you get in here?' I suddenly realised my minder had vanished.

'I walked in. Asked what ward you were on. They told me. I came up in the lift.'

'What about the copper?'

'What copper?'

'Oh, never mind.' I was already tired from the exertion of making conversation but I didn't want him to go. 'I could maybe get you a cup of tea.'

'Could you?'

'We'll have to wait for the nurse.'

'That'd be nice.' He put the bag of grapes on the floor in preparation for his unexpected beverage. It promised to be a small but significant bonus in a life short of such things. In the formality of the setting he was a different person from the one I'd known in the cafe. He was smiling, eager, almost friendly. He was a real old timer with a weighty residue of respect for the institution of the NHS. He'd fought the war for people like me. He was in the artillery: a private with an exaggerated sense of his own unimportance. He talked about it as though it was the happiest time of his life. I asked him why he didn't go to the British Legion. He said it was too painful to be reminded about his youth. As he talked I wondered if I shouldn't have stayed in the army. Perhaps I need those boundary walls to kick against.

After a lull in which I think I might have dropped off to sleep he asked me, 'What will they do to you?' and I then realised why he was there. I had become soap opera to him, he needed the next instalment. But at least his motives were clear.

'They'll charge me. I'll go to prison.'

'I'm sorry.'

'Don't be.' I wanted the nurse to come so I could plead for a cup of tea. I desperately wanted him to have something for coming to see me.

'If there's anything I can do.'

'Do you mean that?' I didn't want to trade on his kindness but there was nobody else.

'Of course I mean it.'

'Find May for me.'

'How?'

'Ask Barry, Hollister. They'll know or they'll be able to find out. But don't say it's for me. Alright?'

'I'll have a bash.'

A nurse flashed past the door, I called out, she came in.

'I don't suppose there's any chance of a cup of tea is there?' I nodded to the old bloke and winked at her. He shuffled on his seat in anticipation.

'You know where the machine is.' She jogged out to continue her errand.

'Sorry,' I said. He shrugged, sorry too. Then the copper came back in, checking his fly.

'What are you doing here?' It was clear that in his eyes my visitors warranted nothing – not even an attempt at politeness. But to give him his credit the old bloke ignored him, winked, picked up the bag of grapes and went without registering he'd even heard the challenge. He didn't look too steady as he hobbled off down the corridor. My bodyguard tried a withering stare before retrieving his chair and stationing it again at the end of the bed.

'Did you score then?' I said.

'None of your business, scumbag.'

And so ended the conversation for another shift. I closed my eyes and tried to get some sleep before the pain grabbed hold again.

# NINETEEN

I FELT BETTER long before I allowed them to notice and when they did they kicked me out and I was driven to John Street police station and charged with kidnapping the baby. It was a first offence, at least the first offence I'd ever been nicked for, but that didn't seem to count for much. I was remanded without bail on the trumped-up charge that they'd found a knife on me during my arrest. I didn't feel so bad about being framed, at least it put me out of the way of any afterthoughts Hollister might have had over not meting out a stiff enough punishment.

After facing the magistrate I was taken downstairs to wait for the prison bus. Two other deadbeats joined me, then an old school type in a faded blazer carrying a greaseproof pack of sandwiches. He began to eat them furtively without offering them around. The smell of fish paste filled the airless room. The man was small and spivvy with slicked-back hair and a ratlike habit of darting a quick look around the room before each mouthful. One of the deadbeats whispered that the bloke was a sex offender – a nonce in prison parlance – and his presence felt like a fitting overture to incarceration: something dark and unspeakable. I learned later why nonces get such a hard time in prison. It's because they're the only life form in there that the other inadequates can safely look down on.

The rat finished his sandwiches, rubbed his hand on his sleeve then offered it to me. 'Brian,' he said. His voice was officer class. I gave him my name in return and then we passed a few uncomfortable minutes like package tourists at an airport waiting for a delayed flight. Neither of us wanted to go into the details of our misdemeanours so we bantered about the surroundings, the weather, the ponce of a magistrate and the type of person who would offer themselves up for such a job. We spat on them all as the deadbeats watched with hostility, then a couple of police officers escorted us to the meat wagon. One of the coppers was much younger than the other. He was the lean one with the pumped-up muscles play-acting the hard man. The older one had the world-weary look of an ageing redcoat.

A doctor examined us when we got to the prison. He'd seen it all of course, like everybody else we came across through reception. He listed ailments and I shook my head. He tapped my chest and looked at my bollocks, then he listened to my heart and after a perfunctory interview to test our sanity we were issued with a bedroll and plastic chamberpot then escorted to the wing to be banged up.

It came as no surprise to discover that prison is crap in all senses of the word. The myth of being buggered every time you stepped into the showers didn't hold up. If anything it was like being in a perpetual playground, but instead of the railings there were walls and a ceiling and the break never ended. It was a factory where vans of food and locked-up men were fed in at one end and nothing came out at the other except unlocked men – a little older, a little harder, rarely wiser or more contrite, and inevitably less capable and with less inclination to earn a living than when they went in. It also seemed to be the only system in the country to have perfected an equal opportunities policy: minorities of all creeds were there in significant numbers.

From the outside Lewes was a beautiful, silent, flint-fronted Victorian lady of a prison. I started off on F Wing and discovered that inside was, of course, quite different. The air was close and tangible and old. The routine was monotonous and relieved only by weekly outings to the magistrates court until the committal proceedings were fixed. That took three months.

I shared a cell with a boy who had used a knife on somebody, a boy called Teddy. He was off his head and night after night I listened to him giving voice to his fevered dreams. He sucked his fingers but always denied it. His face was huge, like a bruised pumpkin; shapeless with skewered eyes and a broken nose. Teddy, like the rest of my colleagues, was a fully paid up member of the No Future brigade. Masturbation and soft drugs were the commonest forms of entertainment in there with weightlifting, table tennis and hard drugs tying for a close second. Buggery brought up the rear.

I began to close down. I shut off my senses one by one just so that I could survive. I began to feel like a mole peering down a long warm tunnel. Outside ... well, there was no outside. Inside was comfortable but as unchallenging and unyielding as a closed fairground on a winter Sunday. My legal-aid solicitor remarked on the change in me. He was a hurried, flustered youth in perpetual disarray with a trailing belt on his green mac and a sheaf of papers that threatened to spill from his arms and scatter in his wake like a hare on a paperchase. I didn't hold out much hope with him preparing my brief. But he seemed confident he could get the kidnapping and assault charges dropped if I'd agree to a guilty plea on the lesser charge of unlawful abduction. We met periodically in the smoky, segregated booths of 'the visits' – a huge library of human interest stories re-enacted daily by the boys on remand. Each day the conversations between the pale faces on one side of the partitions and the concerned parents or wife and bawling child on the other echoed to the rafters and fell back down like a thousand broken promises.

I'd joined the army of blue and white striped shirts, grateful to merge anonymously with the others. At first I felt way out of my depth. By my age it was expected I'd already done a bit of bird and should have been better versed in the codes of the place. The limited hours of association were no pleasure except for the relief they afforded from Teddy's monotonous vaudeville routine of football, fucking birds, headbanging music, motorbikes, and more football. Sometimes he lapsed into quiet introspection but these moments were rare. The landing television was bad for him. Anything with children in it set him off. Either he went misty-eyed and retreated to his bunk and his headphones, or gave some stick to the screws or whoever else was unfortunate enough to be on the landing at the time.

The telly on the landing was useless as a distraction. Television is not a mass spectator sport, especially when each glimpse of female flesh provokes a predictable call and response from the pantomime audience. Bang-up was early so the opportunities for erotic viewing were limited to the presenters on children's television and the occasional pert newsreader. Every Sunday we were escorted to chapel. Nobody there was looking for God, but it functioned as a market bazaar where you could trade tobacco, drugs or anything else of value with blokes from the convicted wing.

The place was full of West Indians. I made the acquaintance of one guy called Peter; he was tall and slow and gentle. We spent a couple of evening associations in his cell sharing a few pipes of hash. But Teddy spoilt it by bullying his way in and forcing a confrontation over something Peter had supposedly hoisted from his collection of comics. Peter hadn't the heart for violence and Teddy's attack frightened him. The next time we met he froze on me and we never spoke again. But Teddy's response to him clarified something I'd been feeling for a while: that he was jealous, that he wanted me for himself. It wasn't a sexual thing, but like a demanding child, he just needed my undivided attention.

Teddy had a small collection of natural history magazines which he would flick through each day searching out pictures of elephants.

'Cliff,' he said one night after lights out. At that moment I was thinking of May, staring into the darkness to try and conjure up an image of her.

'Yes, Teddy.'

'I read this thing, right.'

'Yes.'

'About animals, right?'

'Yes.'

'They reckon each animal and every human has the same number of heartbeats in its life.'

'I didn't know that.'

'Even though the hearts beat at a different speed.'

'Amazing.'

'Makes you think, doesn't it?'

'Yes it does.'
'Goodnight, Cliff.'
'Goodnight, Teddy.'
If nothing else, at least I got an education in there.

After three months of weekly visits to the magistrates' court I was finally committed to the Crown Courts for sentencing on a guilty plea. To my relief, the assault charges had been dropped and the kidnapping charge reduced to that of being an accessory to unlawful abduction. When the day came for sentencing I felt a huge weight of self pity come out of the morning for me. It swooped when we drove past a woman pushing a pushchair. The child in it had angled its head back and was staring at the woman who was soothing him with words of comfort. Inside the court I caught sight of the old bloke in the gallery. He waved but I wondered why he'd bothered to show. He hadn't visited me since I'd been inside, I guess I'd been written out of his soap for a while. He looked worse than when I'd seen him in the hospital. He had a bag of sweets on his knee which he dipped into while he kept his face fixed on the action. The press was there too – it must have been a quiet week newswise – it seemed that they were going to take the opportunity for some more righteous indignation over the supposed kidnap.

My barrister surprised me by speaking eloquently in my defence. I even felt tears coming into my own eyes when he suggested that because of the publicity surrounding the case, I'd already suffered at the hands of the self-appointed judges who had meted out a quite vicious punishment which left me hospitalised. He went on to say I'd been carried along by May and my deep romantic attachment had, to all intents and purposes, temporarily swayed my judgement. The remorse the barrister said I'd felt during my first experience of prison had been yet another burden to bear and he invited the judge to adopt a lenient position.

The judge deliberated for twenty minutes and then came out and pronounced a sentence of three years. The barrister shook my hand and said, 'Good luck.' It was only when I was back in my cubicle in the bus that it hit me. Three years of incarceration. Three years of claustrophobic contact with people like Teddy. Three years of one bath a week and starchy food. Three years of 8 pm lock-ups and 8 am unlocks. Three years without joy. Three years without May.

I was taken back to Lewes prison and found myself on A wing, where I stayed for a month. I expected to be transferred somewhere else in the region, perhaps even an open nick like Ford. But to my surprise I was allocated to C wing at Lewes to serve my sentence there. At moments like that you can find pleasure in the smallest things and I shed some of my cloak of misery when I discovered that I didn't have to share a cell. So I settled to a more solitary routine of quiet, low-key shutdown. Then I got a letter through the censor's office. It was from the old bloke. It was written in pencil on the back of an old Christmas card. I cried like a baby when I read it. Barry was dead.

# TWENTY

There weren't any details. I could barely make out some of the words, the handwriting was so bad. He'd tried to break it gently with carefully chosen phrases like 'he didn't suffer much'; that was the one that stung – 'Much'. How much? I wanted to know. I needed to know. It cut deeper and deeper. I had to know.

The old bloke finished the letter by offering to come and see me. I sent him a visiting order and asked him to get up there as quickly as he could. The waiting was agony. The fact was that Barry was dead. How he'd died shouldn't have mattered. But it did matter. It mattered a lot. I cried over him for a day and a night in my cell. A few landing mates poked their heads round the door and offered tobacco – that's the nearest you get to sympathy in there. I accepted what they offered without thanks and they went without asking for it. Grief has to be private in prison. It spreads quickly if it's not contained and it has to be contained because it breaks the seal on the vacuum and the outside comes rushing in.

By the morning of the second day I'd cried myself to a state of numbness. Something had gone cold inside me. I realised as I was queueing at the hotplate for the inevitable breakfast of semi-solid porridge and fatty bacon that I'd been crying for myself and not for Barry. The revelation surprised me more than it should have done. Tears are always fuelled by self pity, however they're triggered. I cried because Barry was no longer there for me. I cried because the relationship I'd had with him was the longest of my life and that had to mean something. I cried over his new tea set. I cried because I hurt him and I cried because he made me do it.

I needed May to soothe it all away. She was fast becoming the answer to every problem I faced. I fought to stop myself putting her on a pedestal but it was too late, she was no longer mortal but some kind of angel. I went back and back to the evening in the show house, to the scene where she wore the soft perfume and we made love in the dust. That's how I wanted her: sane and solid and controlled. Not the other May, with the gashed lipstick, the free-form thoughts, the sudden tears and anger. But that side had all fallen away. I remember it now but I couldn't cope with it then – in the confinement of the prison, in the eight-by-twelve with the thick old door with its Judas eye.

The old bloke came four days later. I'd half expected him to cry off and when my name was bellowed from the ground floor of the wing after midday bang-up I didn't even hear it. It took my next-door neighbour to call me from my pit before I joined the select few to be escorted for a brief walk across the yard to the visiting room.

The room seemed to be out of scale with the rest of the prison. It was like a small school room with a few tiny chairs lining the back wall and bright posters and toys for the kids. A pair of WRVS women in tight pink perms, fake pearls and fifties twin sets were ineffectually busying themselves round a steaming urn. Beside them a couple of screws sat on a raised stage like guest speakers at speech day. As we were led in, twenty or so conversations suddenly broke out like the first heavy drops of rain in a summer shower.

Before I found the old bloke I caught sight of one of my landing neighbours embracing his wife. A toddler tugged at his leg; he lifted the child to the level of his face and held her against his cheek. As he cried it was easy to forget the other side of him – a bully with a keen eye for the weakest ones on the wing. It was easy to forget everything in the deepening cigarette fog of the visiting room.

The old bloke had his mac on. He'd bought me a cup of tea and a

Kit Kat which he'd put on the furthest side of the small square table. He was cleaning the condensation from his thick glasses with a filthy handkerchief.

'Alright is it?' he asked after we'd shaken hands. I'd wanted to embrace him but I knew he'd have been embarrassed.

'What?'

'The chocolate and tea.'

'Of course.'

'Only – you know . . . ' He pointed towards a sign threatening imprisonment for passing goods to inmates.

'I think we're alright with a Kit Kat. Ta.' He took out a packet of cigarettes, removed one for himself and pushed the packet over. I took one gratefully and he lit it for me, each of us waiting for the other to begin. I decided that it had to be me. 'Look. I appreciate the letter. I really do.'

'I knew they wouldn't tell you.'

'No. They didn't.'

'It was . . . hard, you know. I didn't know how you'd take it. It took me all afternoon to get it right. You get out of the habit of letter writing.'

'Yeah. Well I took it the same way as I would if I'd been on the outside.'

'Yes, well, I didn't know that, did I.'

I felt guilty. I shouldn't have snapped at him but he was talking to me like a child. 'Look. It's alright. I'm coping. Just . . . just be straight with me. Don't worry about it.'

He relaxed a bit, his shoulders dropped an inch and he unbuttoned his coat. 'I never thought you'd go.'

'When?'

'At the beginning. When I said I thought you were thinking about it. I never thought you'd go through with it.'

'Didn't you?'

'If I had a gaff like that. Well . . . '

'Yeah, anyway . . . '

He saw my irritation. We both knew why he was there but he was just limbering up. 'Look, Cliff, there's no other way of saying this. I didn't want to put it in the letter . . .'

But I already knew. 'He killed himself, didn't he?'

'That's right. He killed himself.' He looked shamefaced, as if he should take some of the burden of responsibility. Perhaps it was him complaining about the tea that tipped the balance of Barry's mind.

'How?'

'Does it matter?'

'How? Come on.'

'He, ah . . . he hanged himself.'

'In the flat?'

'Yes.'

'When?'

'When?'

I was ravenous for details. I wanted to know the how, the when, what he was wearing, everything. I didn't need to be told the why. 'Yes. When?'

'It was morning. One morning.'

'When the cafe was open?'

'That's right.'

'And the boy?'

'He was downstairs. Serving.'

'Bastard.'

'He couldn't have done anything.'

'Bastard!'

The screws were over in a flash, one stood at each side of the old bloke to protect him, another came and leaned heavily on my shoulders, pressing me down into the chair.

'It's alright . . . alright.' The old bloke calmed it down, trying to soothe me and them at the same time. 'There's no problem here. He's just had some bad news.' He kept his eyes locked on my face. The screws stayed where they were for a while, waiting for me to go off again. The conversations round the room had all become one-sided. The visitors stared, the inmates went on chatting, it was all too familiar to them.

'I'm alright,' I said. 'I'm sorry.'

'Just watch it or we take you back to the wing. Alright?' The senior screw wagged a podgy finger and waved the other two back to their places. Around the room I sensed a flurry of silent activity subside: some of the visitors had seized the opportunity to pass over their contraband: fags, money, dope.

'I thought you said you could take it.' There was cruelty in the old bloke's face.

'I thought I could.'

'It gets you, doesn't it? You can't prepare yourself for something like that.'

'I never stopped loving him.'

'Didn't you?' The talk of love made the old man uncomfortable. He looked over at the pair on the next table in embarrassment, but they were oblivious to us.

'I didn't mean to hurt him . . . he was too gentle. Too good for his own sake.'

'There were a lot at the funeral.'

'Were there?'

'It was packed. Hollister . . . ' He stopped to gauge my reaction to the mention of his name.

'It's alright.'

'Hollister arranged it. They had the lot. Two cars, flowers . . . they closed up the shops as a mark of respect. He was a well respected man.'

'I know . . . can I?' I pointed to his cigarettes even though I knew he could ill afford to subsidise my habit.

'Yes, go on. They played a pop song at the church.'

'Which one?'

'Something old.'

'He'd have liked that.' Barry was never a churchgoer. His mother used to drag him there as a child. That put him off for life although he did have a grudging admiration for a C of E matinee.

'Only the needle got stuck at the end. Then we went back to the cafe for a sit-down buffet. Hollister said I could come. I asked him and he said it'd be alright. There must have been over a hundred in there. I sat by the window and watched them. The boy brought me a cup of tea over and a sausage roll. He looked after me. I appreciated it. The place was full of nancies but it was alright . . . we made quite an afternoon of it . . . Hollister got drunk . . . I didn't get back till past five. Next door wondered where I'd got to.' He laughed, cagily.

'What about a note? Did he leave anything?'

'Not as far as I know.'

But he didn't need to. Barry wasn't so far off it when I turned on him before I ran away with May. The episode with Hollister's donkeys would have pushed him closer. I may have been the one who took the punishment but I know Barry would have felt the pain of the cuts just as strongly.

My appetite for the details was almost satisfied. But there was one last thing I needed to know. 'Who found him?'

'The boy.'

'Good.'

'You're a cold sod.'

'He could have stopped it.'

'Could he?'

'He could have made him want him then he'd have been alright.'

'Yes, that's right. You blame the boy if it makes you feel better.'

We lapsed into an uncomfortable silence, too close across the table and too unfamiliar with each other for it to be anything else. The woman at the next table was now sitting on the man's lap, they were openly caressing each other. She slid her hand down the front of his shirt, oblivious to their child who had noisily taken control of a tricycle and was now hammering the leg of the table with it.

'The tea's better,' he finally said.

'Is it? The place still open then, is it?'

'For the time being.'

It was all becoming clear. The boy Charlie had muscled in and now he was taking control of the cafe. Little shit. I put him down on my list for retribution when I got out. So far there was . . . but who was I trying to kid? 'I can't do it,' I said.

'What?'

'I can't get angry any more.'
'You seemed to be doing a pretty good job of it a while back.'
'I don't know. I don't know what I feel any more.'
'I know how you feel.' He cocked a smile. 'Here, this'll cheer you up.' He took a letter from his inside pocket and slid it across the table. Luckily the screws didn't see it, otherwise they'd have taken it and given it to the censor. I covered it with my hand.
'May?'
'She wrote to your mate a few weeks ago. He gave it to me. Said I should bring it in if I ever came up here.'
'Barry did?'
'Yes.'
My heart ached for him. I longed for the old bloke to leave so that I could take the letter back to my pit and devour it alone. I touched the envelope, ran my fingers across the front and back of it because I knew that I was connecting with something that May had touched not so long before. The letter was postmarked London and dated four weeks before.
'You going to open it then?'
'No. Later.' I shoved it down the waistband of my trousers and inside my underpants.
He was hurt; reading the letter was his reward for coming to see me but there was no way I could have opened it with him there. 'So, how's life treating you?'
'Don't ask.' The old bloke shook his head mournfully and tutted.
'I am asking.'
'I get very cold. I can't pay the electric so I don't put the fire on much.'
'I'm sorry. I wish I could do something.' Things must have been bad for him, the old bloke belonged to the martyr class. He might have moaned about the small trials of life but he rarely complained about the things that really mattered to him. I never understood whether this was because he belonged to the last generation who got by without help from anyone outside their families or whether he just didn't know how to take sympathy. Either way, it was another indicator of his slow decline.

'It's not down to you, is it? I did my bit for this lot – now it's time they did their bit for me. But they won't. It's not right.'

'It's not.'

He stared me straight in the eye. 'I've had enough now, Cliff.'

'Don't be silly.'

'No . . . there's nothing left for me. I know how your mate felt. I do.'

'Come on. How can you say that?'

'I say it because that's how I feel. I get up in the morning and all I want to do is to go back to bed.'

'It'll get better. Hang on for a month. Things always look worse when the nights are long.' I was trotting out the clichés that I hated hearing myself. Meaningless, comfortless words, for my own benefit, not his. I was impotent to help him so I offered him a glimpse of the future. That's all comfort usually is – a hollow promise of time not yet spent.

'Maybe . . . maybe.' His despair rang out like a church bell. 'So – what else can I tell you?'

'Will you come again?'

'I'll try and get up.'

'I'd appreciate it.'

'What's it like in here?'

'It's alright.'

'Not like you see on the telly though, I bet?'

'No. You won't find Ronnie Barker in here.'

'Do you get scared?'

'I can look after myself.'

He laughed and stood stiffly, buttoning his coat. 'Yes, I can see that.'

'You can stay a bit longer can't you?'

'No. I don't like to be out when it gets dark. I've got to get to the station then get a bus at the other end.'

'Of course.'

'Right then.' He patted his pockets.

'Thanks for coming.'

'You look after yourself.'

We shook hands, he walked to the gate. A screw span his key in the lock and the old bloke disappeared through the visitors' door. He'd left the cigarettes on the table. I slid them next to May's letter and waited to be escorted back to the wing. I never saw him again.

# TWENTY-ONE

I TORE BACK to my cell and wedged up the door so nobody could get in unannounced. Then I opened the pink envelope. The letter was everything I'd hoped for and more. It was newsy and light, all about getting out of the hospital and making a fresh start. She said she was putting everything behind her and looking forward to going back to the cafe and seeing Barry again. And then there was the part that wiped the pain away. 'I hope you don't hate me for taking Cliffie away. I couldn't help it. I love him. Now I'm going to find him and see if he still loves me. I'm sorry if it hurts you, Barry, but I have to be honest. I have had to face up to a lot of things about myself and I now know that I have to stop living how I think other people want me to live. I have to start living for myself. You understand, don't you? But there's something else. I think it's the reason why they let me out early. Can you guess?'

I turned the page. I couldn't guess. I had no clue – but the solution to two riddles leaped out at once: 'I'm pregnant. I'm going to have Cliffie's baby. Isn't it wonderful? I want to sing and cry all at the same time. And Barry, I don't want you to be left out. I want you to be the goddaddy.

'I'll write again soon. Will you write to me and tell me if you've heard from him? I know he's in prison but he won't be in there for ever. I'll write to him in there and perhaps they'll let me see him. All my fondest regards. May.'

I wish you could see that letter. Because then you'd understand why it provoked equal measures of joy and horror. I'd forgotten, or chosen to ignore, the fact that it was Barry she'd written it to and not me. So he'd read it, then re-sealed it. He'd heard the news first, and May's insensitive offer. And he'd responded to it in the only way he knew how: at the bottom of the letter, in pencil, he'd written: 'Goodbye Cliffie' and written two kisses beneath it.

So he did leave a suicide note, except it was a note written for him; a suicide note in somebody else's hand. It was probably the only real act of cruelty in his life. I was left feeling sick but elated, depressed and joyful. I didn't sleep for two days as the struggle between joy at the news of the baby fought against my anger that she'd told Barry first and it had caused his suicide. Then I'd feel angry at him for messing up his life over me, then I'd forgive May because she couldn't have known what the letter was going to do. In the end the living won out over the dead and I settled back to a kind of quiet equilibrium with a warm, slow-burning joy inside me that was never quite there but never too far out of reach: it was a joy that a new life was coming and I was responsible for it; that a wasted, wasteful life was set to have some purpose. It renewed my love for May tenfold.

When I tried to work out the dates, I realised with horror that the baby couldn't be too far off. We'd parted in July, it was then late March which meant that the birth was around a month away. Then another fear took hold of me. The letter was postmarked February and I hadn't heard from her since then. What if something had gone wrong? What if a letter had gone astray? What if they weren't letting me have any letters from her? I realised with a jolt that she probably thought I already knew the news. After all, she'd written the letter that Edie had intercepted, she must now be wondering why I hadn't responded. Perhaps she thought I didn't care or, worse, wanted nothing more to do with her. This is the real punishment of incarceration. It not only strips you of your freedom but it also puts you at the mercy of a system designed to stop you connecting with the outside world. That's fine if the connections are not worth maintaining – and many are in prison for that reason – but if they are you're in deep trouble. So all I could do was to write to the address on the letter in the hope that she was still there and that she'd respond.

It was hard to get the right tone into it. I didn't want to frighten her off by being too heavy but I wanted to convey my fears and some of the urgency that I was feeling. When I'd finished the letter, I re-read it several times. Each time I did it gave off a different meaning. Finally it made no sense at all so I wrote another and then sent it off before I changed my mind again. I also sent a short note to Edie, throwing myself at her mercy and asking her to return May's letter to me. All I could then do was to try and penetrate the bureaucracy. I buttonholed the Assistant Governor on one of his jaunts round the wing and told him what the situation was. Passing the buck as usual, he told me to put in to see the chaplain. He explained that I had no rights at all but suggested that I pray for divine guidance. In the meantime he put my name down on the list for a prison visitor. One Friday evening, during association, an inadequate, lardy character arrived and informed me that he was my prison visitor and would do anything he could for me. Then he talked about himself and his dry-cleaning company for an hour. I don't know why he considered the fact relevant to the situation but it pumped him up giving me the information. I choked back my anger and managed to get a promise out of him that he'd try and trace May. But I knew it was hopeless, he hadn't even bothered to write anything down, all he was interested in was coming to see the animals in the zoo. Prison visitors are the worst species of humanity – worse even than screws who at least don't pretend to be something they're not.

I took up gym to alleviate the burden of the hours on the wing. C Wing is a tall, narrow, warehouse with four stacked shelves of landings on each side. Suicide netting is strung between the 'ones' – the first-floor landings. It's dotted with dirty laundry, towels and fag packets. The characteristic inmate pose is to be seen with hands clenched together, foot up on the bottom rail, wrists on the top rail, gazing down at the wing. From beneath it looks as if you're staring up at the side of a huge liner with the passengers staring arrogantly back. The place is artificially too bright but it feels closed down. There's a perpetual atmosphere of hopeful anticipation that something will come along to break the monotony. But when it does, it's usually nothing more than scattered shuffles, cries from the screws or the sudden ringing of alarm bells. Time weighs heavily, but after a while it ceases to have any absolute meaning. Daylight is something glimpsed through small windows and sometimes encountered in the tiny exercise yard. Night begins at bang-up at 8 pm and goes on for ever. You can scrutinise a minute and it'll last all day. Sometimes days seem to last no more than minutes. Dope and the other chemical companions are the only relief, but they distort the time frame further.

But, like I'd said to the old bloke, it really wasn't so bad in there. At least it wasn't until I got the letter from May. That put a timescale on things, a timescale out of kilter with the one that was governing my life. With each day that passed my fear grew that I'd lost contact with her. I was also afraid that she'd have to face the birth alone and, if she did go off the rails, the baby would be put into care and I'd have no rights over it.

A month passed. Time hung heavy as the wind whipped past and the rain drummed on the small cell window. The wind is called on by poets and writers to represent many things but to me it was a constant cruel reminder of my night on the pier with May as we danced together and heard the child wailing against the waves. Perhaps it was a premonition. It might just as well have been.

I put down to see the governor. He was polite and sympathetic but it seemed that he wasn't allowed to bend the rules for the likes of me. He was a fast-track civil servant on his way up the shit pile. I was scum. I could have taken honesty but I couldn't take being patronised, and I said so. Then I lashed out and found myself pinned to the floor by two burly screws. 'I expected better of you,' the governor said, buttoning up his tweed jacket, running his finger round his tight collar. It seemed we'd let each other down in that respect.

So the days came and went and I saw many of them out down the block. The screws couldn't take the change in me. I'd been a model prisoner, now I was a maniac they all gave a wide berth to when we passed on the corridors. But they'd seen it happen before: I'd flipped my lid and smashed up everything in my cell. Easy for them to pass judgement, they could go home at night and see the place with fresh eyes in the morning. The irony was that most of them had served longer in the nick than any of the inmates and were just as damaged by the system as we were. But they wouldn't see it when I shouted the simple truth at them. They just kicked out a little harder when they bundled me to the block.

Two things happened in April. First, I got a letter from May. It was dated two weeks after I'd written to her, and it was from an address in Dorset. It was clear from what she wrote that she hadn't received my letter. This was a different May, a May I didn't recognise. She'd been 'doing some work on herself' – whatever the hell that meant. It seemed she'd fallen in with some hippies and they'd got to her just at the right time. She was living in a huge house in Dorset with a gaggle of kids, eight or nine assorted parents and a fleet of VW vans parked outside. None of the kids looked to any particular adults as their parents – the group 'parented' all the kids, the kids in turn 'parented' the adults. There was somebody called 'Kit' who'd taken her in. Bastard! I could picture him – nearly bald but with a greasy ponytail, NHS glasses and three earrings up his left ear, a pair of rank sandals and obligatory blue jeans, kaftan and halitosis. I wanted to kill him. I wanted to kick his bollocks into orbit.

I lifted the weights in the gym with a passion. Now I had a reason. Kit was the reason. Kit was going to steal my child from me before I even had a chance to see him – or her. I decided I was going to tear him limb from limb, swing him round with his ponytail and send him crashing through the flap in his bloody wigwam.

I got into a fight with a boy on the landing. A thick spastic-grimaced full-blown cretin of a boy who'd been pissing me about over some tobacco he owed me. I went for him and kicked and bit and gouged until I'd torn three kinds of living shit out of him. The blokes on the wing were placing bets on how long he was going to stay conscious. If the screws hadn't dragged me off I would have killed him. They took me down the block again, stripped me and trussed me up. I screamed at the walls. I screamed again and again and a screw banged the door. I screamed at him and Hollister and Barry and Enright and after half an hour of screaming I felt better. I didn't want to kill Kit any more. I just wanted to maim him. Badly.

But who was this new May? She'd been 'thinking'. That wasn't like her. The May I knew was a creature of pure instinct, of pure emotion, driven by irrational desires and overwhelming needs. Anyway, thinking, it seemed, had led her to wondering, and wondering had led her to considering the possibility that as I hadn't replied to her letters then she could only assume I wasn't interested and she hoped I'd be happy with my choice but she had to make a home for herself and her new baby.

So my letter hadn't reached her and the only reason hers had reached me was that she'd sent it care of the cafe and the boy had forwarded it. I'd been defeated by the system and the only option I had was to try and write to her again – this time in the hope that it would get to her in her new home in Dorset before the baby was born.

I tried to control it when I wrote. I told her that I wasn't looking for anything any more. That all I wanted was her and our child and if she looked deep within herself and got all of that hippy mumbo-jumbo out of her system then she'd feel the same thing. But that didn't feel right, so I tore it up and started again, this time more sober and rational. That didn't work either. I had to convey some of the anger I was feeling. I spent all day composing a page and at the end of it tore it to shreds. The night was the same. And the next day. I couldn't eat, I couldn't sleep. I ended up weeping out of frustration. I felt her and the baby slipping away from me. But I knew I couldn't let her go. With Barry gone, May was the only one who made sense of it, who got me through the long nights.

I remember the date I had the dream. It was April the 12th. May had had the baby and it was a boy and I watched it all from the door of the delivery room. But I couldn't get close to her because she was surrounded by leather-clad bikers. And when the child was born they held it high and carried it from the room and May was left lying, alone, and I wanted to reach out and touch her but I couldn't because I was watching her through the cell window. And that was it. At the time I was convinced our child was born on that night.

When I woke the next day I was broken. A lifer popped his head round the door to see what was wrong. I didn't care any more. I just didn't care who saw. The façades in there are all so thin you can punch through them in an instant; like the crust on a pie they crack easily to reveal the hot bubbling brown mess beneath. The lifer seemed concerned. I told him to fuck off. He didn't take any notice. If I wanted to cut myself that was my business, nobody else's. It was my leg, my arm. Who had the right to tell me I couldn't inflict damage on my own body?

He came in carefully like he was cornering a rabid dog. Yes, the cell was smashed up. Yes, there was shit on the walls, maybe on me, but it was up to me how I decorated it – you just don't walk into somebody's room without permission. That's one of the first rules you learn. But that bastard was walking in without my say so. Jesus, what a day it was turning out to be. Then he slipped on something: the blood. The blood was pretty thick by then. It was pulsing from my wrist like a spring from a hillside. It ran onto my fingers and down onto the bedding, and from there to the floor where it was congealing. Bloody Kit. Bloody cunt Kit bastard.

'Hey . . . ' The lifer started cooing at me like a child (a tall guy – gaunt and grey faced like an undertaker early for his appointment).

'Fuck off.'

'Cliff . . . isn't it?'

'You can just . . . ' Somebody else came in. Somebody behind him like in the car park. Like that hot cold night in the car park when Hollister's bullies left me in the trolley. 'Leave me alone.'

'Is that what you want?'

'Yes.'

'Sure?'

'Yes. Leave me.'

At least . . . at least in there the blokes understand. The one thing you have left is the control over your destiny. Authority straps you down and makes you impotent in every area but the one that really matters: if you want to take your own life then you can. But they have to be sure you mean it. Anger, self-loathing, frustration are too often the triggers in there so those who have been round long enough come to recognise the signs: experts in despair; the only ones left in the country who still have the power to pass the death sentence. Why can't you kill yourself by holding your breath? Because we'd all be dead.

An alarm bell sprang to life but it was distant, probably from another wing. But by then I didn't feel so bad. I just wanted to be left alone in my cell. Left alone to die by a riverbank. Then the bell was crying in another world – echoing curiously in the roof of a long-dead pier, in a cathedral, tinkling in a Himalayan temple on a goat-grazed hill – but May never came, she never came, never came . . . the room spun and slowed, spun and slowed and the weight rose from my chest to my throat and the warmth drained from my body. If you want to know how it feels, this is how it feels; a slow distancing, a safe, solid, heavy-centred slipping away from it all. White warmth. A white corridor. But even through it all I am aware of the reproving look from the fat screw as he waddles in and tots up the paperwork he is going to have to fill in. But it's just another cell death. Another cell empty. There's room in this womb for another dead baby. Come on in, the water's lovely.

# TWENTY-TWO

'HE'S DEAD.'

'Bang them all up.'

'No pulse. Can't find a . . . '

'Have you . . . '

'Doc.'

' . . . his way.'

'fucken stink.'

' . . . bloody mess . . . bucket . . . '

'AG?'

'Today?'

'Saw him yesterday was it?'

'No . . . '

'Day off. Leave, always on leave when you need . . . '

'Bangor. Booked it with the family.'

'How long?'

'Ten minutes, doc.'

'More. Maybe more.'

'Give me a hand here.'

'He's dead.'

'Are you pronouncing death?'

'No . . . I . . . '

'Roll him.'

' . . . Topped himself . . . '

'Take this. Put some pressure on here.'

'Bloody mess . . . '
'Harder please.'
'Stretcher . . . '
'Will you please . . . '
'Sorry, doc.'
'Stretcher!'
' . . . anyway, Steph wanted to know . . . '
'Make way.'
'Dead is he?'
'Has the ambulance arrived?'
'Holding it at the gates.'
'Do they want this man to die?'
'Probably.'
'Formalities.'
'Not dead then is he . . . '
'A weak pulse.'
'Sandy was saying to Steph.'
' . . . doesn't mean he didn't bring the money even if . . . '

You won't believe this but I was watching all this from above. Something was stopping me going through the ceiling but at the same time preventing me falling to the floor. A force suspended me – but it wasn't really me. Not the balls and sockets and blood and gore. All of that was lying on the floor. What remained of me was the essence; the soul, if there is one, the life force in a take-away doggy bag pinned to the ceiling of the cell. And it was watching the scene dispassionately, waiting either to be called back and plugged in or to be despatched somewhere to join a long happy smiling queue of white-suited dead people outside the celestial way station.

'Thank God that's all over,' says a smiling blood-drenched torso.
'Laugh, I nearly died,' says a woman who choked on a fish bone.
'What happens now?' says the first one.
'Don't know, it feels like I've been waiting here for ever.'
'Perhaps this is Hell then – a queue.'
'No. It's not a queue, we're just walking slowly.'

But that doctor knew his stuff. The queue suddenly disappeared and I found myself lying on my back on the floor like a thrown wrestler. It felt like a dress rehearsal for something else but at least next time I knew I wouldn't go in cold.

The next two years flew past. Each day was pretty much like the last and the further April receded into the past the less anxious I became about May and my child. I heard nothing from her and although I made the occasional enquiry through my welfare officer I got nothing new in the way of information. So I turned down the heat. My attempt at suicide had heartened me. Although I'd failed to achieve the final solution to my despair I knew that if necessary I could easily pull it off the next time. I'd just have to pick a better moment. So in a small way I'd won a victory over my captors, I had the means of escape within my grasp and there was nothing they could do about it. Ironically, knowing this was the only thing that kept me from topping myself.

But I hadn't given up on May. I refused to believe that we didn't have a future together. So I constructed a fragile castle of hope in which she and my child waited – alone, pining, but secretly convinced that I would soon be there to rescue them.

I was released one June morning, stepping gingerly into a world speeding quickly past. I was told to expect it, but the pace of life outside the gates took me by complete surprise – as did the starkness of the colours. The only item of value I carried with me on the out was the letter with May's address on it, and that became my destination. But first I decided to go back into Brighton and collect what few belongings I had left at the cafe. I knew deep down that this was just a pretext for going there. I wanted to convince myself that Barry was really dead and that his suicide hadn't been cooked up as some cruel hoax by Hollister. I also wanted to see the place where it had happened so I could fix it in my brain and rid myself of the constant nightmares I was having about it.

I hitched a lift the short distance back to the coast and the town greeted me with unfurled flags as I sailed in on the coat-tails of a breeze. The town recognised me, I could tell, because the sun cried out a greeting and the air was clear and even the rusting trellis of the ruined pier looked strangely beautiful.

'Ta mate, this'll do.' I leaped from the step of the lorry by the pier and skipped through the dense traffic to the other side of the prom. I grasped the tubular railings, the sun was a heavy overcoat, I could see kids on the beach, the colours were all primary, everything was beautiful. The day was as good as the first day at Barry's. I wanted to swim, to wash off all the accumulated dirt of the last two and a half years, to do something for which I had to ask no permission.

I left my clothes on the beach and plunged headlong into the water. A dog came from nowhere and snapped at my heels. I struck out towards the horizon and immediately felt the benefit of my long hours in the gym. The water released me and felt fresh even though it was not. In prison the water tastes and feels second-hand, as though it has passed through the body at least once. But then I began to tire, turned and swam back to the shore where I padded painfully back across the pebbles to my clothes which the mutt was sniffing. A kick sent him off. I dressed and lay on a bed of pebbles to soak up the sun.

I didn't sleep but concentrated on the sea crashing in front of me. Behind, the traffic set up a constant bass rumble along the coast road. Snatches of conversation added fluted melodies. I could have stayed there for the rest of the day but I felt drawn back to the cafe. After more than two years another hour or so shouldn't have mattered, but somehow it did, so I sprang to my feet and walked along the shoreline in the direction of the other pier.

The boy saw me the moment I walked into the cafe. He smiled. It seemed incongruous in the setting. I hadn't yet grieved for Barry in the one place I'd really known him and I knew I still had to lay him to rest in my mind. I couldn't face going straight up to the flat so I slid onto a seat by the window. The boy poured out a coffee from a hissing gizmo on the counter and came over. The place had been completely refashioned in a mock-deco style. It was all smoked mirrors and stainless steel, curves and bronze figurines holding white globes. Even the menus were blocked out in thirties script and decorated with black silhouetted figures in evening dress. I knew the old bloke would have hated it. I wondered where he was; I'd neither seen nor heard from him since he'd come to visit me.

'Cliffie.' The boy put the coffee in front of me and slid into the booth opposite. That was something else, the old scuffed melamine tables had been replaced by matt black booths.

'Charlie, isn't it?'

'That's right. I thought you were about due . . . I expected you to walk through that door any day.'

'And here I am.'

'I kept your stuff upstairs.'

'Good of you.' The irony was hard to mask, I didn't know why I was even bothering to try. Then I recognised that I was feeling guilty over something but I couldn't quite pin down what it was.

'Like it?' The boy swept his hand round the room.

'No. It's horrible.'

'Hollister did it.'

'I can believe that. What's it got to do with him anyway?'

'He took it over when Barry . . . look, come up.' He stood up, barking his knee on the edge of the table. He'd put on weight and lost some of his freshness. His eyes seemed duller and sadder. Something had died in him.

'I'll come up in a minute.'

'Right.' He moved slower too, perhaps it was just age. He certainly wasn't pretty any more.

I lit up and looked for an ashtray. An eager girl came over and slid one across the table with a genuine smile. I smiled back. When Charlie returned to the counter she took it as permission to hover and swap small talk.

'Still nice?' She craned her neck to indicate that she was talking about the outside world.

'Lovely. Lovely and warm.'

'Too nice to be in here anyway.' She rubbed the shoulders of her thin cardigan and mimed feeling chilly.

'Have you been working here long?'

'A year – almost. A year last month.' She was the sort of woman who would have known the exact date, probably even time, that she'd begun, but she spared me the finer details.

'What about Hollister. Do you see much of him?'

'Mr Hollister, yes.' She clarified, 'He's always been a gentleman to me.' Funny how the victims of Hollister's cruelty always ended up defending him. It was a mark of the fear he inspired.

'He owns the place then?'

'Think so – yes.' But she'd been distracted by someone across the street. She started waving frantically and mouthed something about 'tonight' through the glass. A clone of her mouthed something back.

'I'm going up,' I said.

'Wha . . . ? Oh, yes. Right, love. Know the way?'

'Yes thanks.'

But I didn't. I went behind the counter to where the staircase should have been and found myself in the kitchen where a man and what looked to be a dwarf were manically chopping carrots. The dwarf finished with a flourish; they both laughed and started on the next batch. I went back into the cafe.

'That way, love.' The woman pointed to a new door on the right of the room marked 'Toilets'. It gave onto a short spray-scented corridor with a lino floor and a new wooden staircase. I went up.

Charlie was in the old living room which seemed to have become an office. The chairs and settee were strewn with cardboard boxes and piles of envelopes; Hollister had obviously hi-jacked it for one of his dodgy direct-mail ventures. The boy was sitting at a white desk scanning a sheet of paper self-consciously. He looked up, feigning surprise, but I knew he would have heard me coming up the stairs.

'Sit down, Cliffie.' He leaped up like a nervous host and shifted a box from the settee. I declined the offer.

'Where's Barry's stuff?'

'Gone.'

'All of it?'

'Most of it. It wasn't much . . . I mean what was the point of keeping it all?'

I shifted a pile of boxes from beside the fireplace and was glad to see that Barry's paperbacks were still there – dusty but untouched. In front of them was one of his deco tea cups growing mould. 'Hollister chucked it all, did he?'

'Yes.'

'Nice man.'

'I've known worse.'

'God help you.'

'Sit down. Please.'

I felt tense with the closeness of the room and the proximity to where it had all happened. Even with much of his stuff gone there was still enough of Barry in that room to make it feel as though he was still around.

'Go on, sit down.'

I sat on the settee, my coat across my lap. I felt like a nervous interviewee.

Charlie said, 'How have you been?'

'Mustn't grumble. How about you?'

'Do you need money?'

'A couple of thousand wouldn't go amiss.'

'I could manage fifty.'

'I bet you could.'

'It wasn't my fault, you know.'

'You said you'd look after him.'

'I did.'

'Bloody good job you made of it, didn't you.'

'Like you did, you mean . . . It wasn't my fault.'

'Course it wasn't.' I choked back the bitterness.

'When you went he just . . . he died then you know. There was nothing I could do for him. It was like living with a ghost.'

'Christ.'

'It's hard living with someone like that. Someone without hope. But I tried. I'm not perfect but I tried.'

I couldn't stay angry at him. I was really only angry at myself. But you can't turn anger on yourself unless you try self-murder, and I couldn't even do that properly. It seemed that someone was trying to protect me from myself. I wondered why. Perhaps it was because there was going to be a time when I was going to have a part to play in the greater scheme of things. To reach out and save a child from a speeding car who was to become the mother of the father of the man who saved the world from crashing into the sun. Yes, there is a God. The patterns are too complicated and fragile for the world to be left to its own devices. The watchmaker watches the mechanism through a long glass, occasionally dropping oil onto seized parts, sometimes twisting others out of true for sheer devilment. The watchmaker cares for the watch, but his concern with the fragile parts inside extends only so far as to make sure they keep the hands turning.

'Charlie,' I said.

'Yes?' He looked up from his shoes.

'It wasn't your fault.'

He cried then, maybe for the first time. I went over and held him. He didn't stand but, like the old man many months before, clung onto my waist and vented his pain into my chest. Then he looked up to the ceiling. I followed his eyes. He was staring at an old hook that once suspended a favourite swinging chair. The chair went to the dump one spring clean but Barry was always set against taking the hook down – he said it might come in useful one day – a hook sunk securely into a joist.

The boy said, 'We could go to the cemetery if you'd like.'

'No. Let's go and get pissed.' He smiled and his rosy face lit up like the face on the old fruit gums packets; a cocky insolent smile just the wrong side of innocence: a smile to break a mother's heart.

We walked into town and chose a pub by the station. We took a couple of stools by the bar and the landlord kept discreetly in the background but was always within earshot when we called for a drink. I stuck with Scotch, Charlie went for the vodka and we drank thirty quid away as the afternoon wore on.

Then we went back to the cafe. The woman had shut up shop and left a curt note in a childish hand on the counter; something about people being inconsiderate and her going out tonight and Charlie having known about it for ages. Anyway, we had a laugh at the spellings, then fell into the kitchen and pantomimed cooking a meal.

We managed to get something warm onto the plates and took them through into the cafe. The place looked better at night, less trashy, almost serene. We left off the main lights and illuminated the globe on our table. It took me straight back to the night on the pier when me and May cruised round the arcade and ended up possessing it. Beyond the glow of the table light there was nothing.

Afterwards, we went to bed. The booze had taken the edge off my need such as it was, and, despite the boy's caressing, his hot childlike breath on my face, all I wanted was to sleep. Prison had closed me down in all sorts of ways and I knew it would take a more tender heart than his to awaken whatever was left inside me. Instead we clung together and slept safely through the night.

When I woke the sun was shining through the thin curtains and the boy was downstairs. I dressed to an echo of another encounter and went down for my breakfast. I had one more score to settle before leaving the town for good, finding May, and seeing if we had anything left between us.

# TWENTY-THREE

I ATE BREAKFAST in the cafe. The boy looked well hung-over but I felt fine. He'd already planned our futures together. Life was a series of rude awakenings to him; he nipped at crumbs of kindness and misinterpreted them as commitment, poor little sod. Anyway, I put him right as gently as I could and he took it pretty well. I also found out that the old bloke was still around, not in the best of health, but mobile, so I put him on the day's agenda of fond farewells. Then I went back up to take a last look around the flat.

My stuff was in a cardboard box in May's old room. I sifted through it but I could find nothing worth keeping except for one old photograph of Barry. He was standing outside the cafe with his arms crossed like a butcher in an old sepia print. The photo was from just before we'd met – or perhaps just after; he looked young and full of hope. I kept the picture and put the rest of the stuff with the other bagged rubbish on the landing, then I had a poke round Barry's room. His wardrobe and drawers were empty. Hollister had done as good a job of eradicating him as Barry did to May. I looked up to see the boy watching me from the door, bored now by it all, wanting me away.

'Alright then,' he teased.

'Alright what?'

'I'll tell you.'

'Tell me what?'

'It won't make any difference, I suppose. Though I don't really see why I should.'

'What are you talking about?' It looked like the previous night's jaunt had affected his state of mind as well as his complexion.

He went into the sitting room and came out with a crumpled rag of paper which he thrust at me saying, 'Read it.' I reached for it but then he snatched it away. 'It's from Barry.'

'To me?'

'That's right.' He handed it over and left me to read it alone. It was a scrawl; a hurried, last-minute postscript, jotted sometime between putting down his cup of tea and tightening the noose round his neck. There was no camp drama in it, which said a lot about his state of mind at the time. I knew he'd have regretted it: his one big chance to play the matinee queen and he'd thrown it all away. The note had only ten words on it: 'Cliff, I'm sorry. I want you to have the cafe.'

So it seemed he'd had a change of heart after sending on the letter from May. Not enough to impinge on his despair, but sufficient to try and cushion the blow. The note was a real eye-opener, I never knew he owned the cafe. I'd always imagined he'd got it on a short lease, which raised the inevitable question of what right Hollister had to take it over.

'Charlie!' I shouted.

He came back in, having anticipated my first thought. 'He won't let you have it.'

'Why not?'

'He threw the note away. I got it out of the bin. He laughed when he read it.'

'Over me or Barry?'

'What's the difference? Over you, I should think. Barry was still swinging when he got here – even Hollister's not that callous.'

'I appreciate you saving it for me.'

'Yeah. Anyway, I don't suppose it'll make any difference.'

'We'll have to see. Where does he work from now?'

'Usual place.'

'Right. Look, thanks for this.'

'Be careful, Cliffie.'

'Goodbye, Charlie.'

'Might see you around then.'

'Yeah.'

We shook hands then I went down the back staircase and onto the road with the lock-up garages in it. I looked up and saw him staring out of the window. He wasn't looking at me, he was craning his neck as though any minute he was expecting someone to come round the corner; someone new, someone who'd stay for a while. It wasn't until I'd turned the corner that I realised I'd been watching Charlie in the window and not Barry.

I took a taxi to the old bloke's house but I couldn't raise anybody at the front door. The place was set in the middle of a bleak windblown council estate on the edge of town. The garden had gone back to nature, the bedroom window was part-boarded, a row of filthy milk bottles lined the step. I walked round to the back. Next door was blasting rock music through the wall. A baby was screaming, a dog barking with excitement. I peered in. The place was stacked with newspapers; hundreds of them in the kitchen, the dining room, every room I peered in to. There was just enough space for him to pass between the waist-high piles; it looked like a grid of first world war trenches.

I knocked on the back door, again there was no reply. Then a woman came out from next door, her hair in a floral towel, a plastic basket of washing under her arm.

'Not in?' she said.

'No. He alright, is he?'

'You a friend?'

'Yeah.'

'He's alright.'

'Keep an eye on him, do you?'

'I try. He borrows the phone sometimes for the doctor. I suppose we'd know something was wrong if we didn't see him for a few days. But my husband works nights, you see.'

I was defeated by her logic. 'Right . . . Tell him Cliffie called, will you.'

'Oh – you were the one in prison, weren't you.' She pulled her basket closer to her breast.

'That's right.'

'I'll tell him. He'll probably be back soon. He doesn't go far nowadays.'

'Thanks.'

I was pleased he was alright and that he wasn't totally alone. The woman with the dog and the baby and the husband on nights – she'd keep an eye on him. You could tell she cared more than she was prepared to admit. I liked the look of her. I said goodbye and got a cab to Hollister's office.

Hollister rented a couple of rooms over a bookshop which he always claimed lent him legitimacy. A secretary tried to stall me at the top of the narrow stairs by saying he wasn't in but his old camel coat was on a peg by the door and his aftershave hung in the air like a blast of fly spray. I told her I'd wait and she prissily pointed to a plastic orange chair by the wall. The place looked as though it had been furnished with the off-casts from a company that had gone under in the sixties. Everything was a faded government-surplus grey and coffee cup-ringed. The photocopier was enormous, the computer on the desk trailed dangerous cables to a ramshackle printer on a card table. The place had the air of a small, down-at-heel detective agency. The only colour in the room came from a pornographic calendar showing two naked women attending to each other over the bonnet of a Ford Fiesta. It provoked the same sickening heart-lurch you get when you drive past a traffic accident.

The secretary must have buzzed Hollister because he came out as soon as I sat down and frightened her into a spate of coffee-making before drawing me into his office. The room was dominated by a desk and a drinks cabinet. Beneath the reek of his aftershave was the staler reek of a recent fart.

'Well,' he said, looking me up and down as he sank into his revolving leatherette executive armchair.

'Well well,' I said, taking a lower chair across the desk from him.

'You look . . . ah . . . ' He reached for the word.

'Older?'

'That's it, Clifford. Older. More mature. Prison obviously suited you.'

'It wasn't so bad.'

'I had an inkling you'd thrive in there. Anybody with an ounce of wit could do worse than a short spell of incarceration to hone his talents.'

'You should try it.'

'Oh I have . . . I have . . . ah, coffee . . . ' The secretary came nervously in, another victim of Hollister's regime of quiet brutality. He took the plastic beakers from her and dismissed her with a flick of his wrist. 'Useful girl. Very discreet. Not averse to a few hostess-type duties. Get my drift?' He winked a moist bloodshot eye.

'The new wife, is it?'

'Droll. Very droll.'

That one went in past his guard. Hollister's ex-wife was a notorious good-timer but was alleged to be the only person he ever felt anything for. He walked in on her one night just as she and a business partner of his were enthusiastically sealing a deal across the office desk. It was the end of his association with the opposite sex and the introduction to a course of plastic surgery for both her and the businessman.

'So what brings you back to Brighton? Are you here to offer your talents?'

'No, I'm strictly self-employed now. Should I choose to ply my trade it'll be on my behalf.'

'And what would that trade be, I wonder? A proclivity for petty vandalism, assault and shagging members of both sexes hardly constitutes a full CV.'

'It never did you any harm.'

'Oh, Cliffie. You've become a cynic. You've lost your . . . joie de vivre. Where did it go, I wonder?'

'Some of it in a supermarket car park. A little more on the floor of a prison cell.'

'Yes. I heard about that. And I have to say I was surprised. I've always seen you as an optimist – hardly the hallmark of a suicide.'

'Depends on your religion, doesn't it?'

'Not how I understand it, no. But, religion, you've found yourself a new hobby, have you?'

'You should try it. Give you something to do on Sunday mornings, make you happier.'

'Happiness is the prerogative of the feeble-minded, as well you should know by now.'

'That's good. I thought I was missing out on something.'

'I've missed you, Clifford.'

'Me too.'

'That's nice.'

'But I won't miss next time.'

He wasn't sure about me. I wasn't sure about him any more. Hollister's days were numbered, the signs were everywhere. Charlie had told me a pair of Iranian brothers had set their sights on his territory. Hollister was out of touch with modern street warfare. He'd served his time in the last of the razor gangs, when there was still a recognised code of conduct. But society had changed since then, the accepted order had broken down from the top to the bottom. The new boys carried artillery and were conspicuous consumers – they wore Armani, drove Porsches and financed their scratch armies with the proceeds from the drugs trade. Hollister's protection scams seemed mild in comparison with the flashing-light moments and the blighted futures the new boys were pushing.

'You paid for the funeral.' I went on the offensive.

'Correct.'

'Thank you.'

'It was the least . . . '

'You took it out of the proceeds of the cafe, did you?'

'Clifford, please remember where you are.'

'I thought I knew where I was last night. I thought I was in your cafe. Then I woke up this morning and found out it was mine.'

'I have dreams like that.'

'I know you do. I've got Barry's note.'

'Have you?'

'And according to a solicitor acquaintance it's legally binding. You have no right to the cafe. I'll take you to court for it.'

'Very amusing.'

'You think I wouldn't?'

'What do you think? Only the very poor and the very rich have access to the legal system. And only the latter category when it comes to litigation.'

'I could make a nuisance of myself.'

'Yes, that does seem to be rather a speciality of yours. Look, Clifford, why are we talking like this? I thought we were supposed to be friends.'

'So did I.'

'Then you mustn't let our recent difficulties get in the way of that. I'm generous to my friends, you know that.'

It was becoming clear. Hollister had lost his appetite for it all. He seemed duller and more shapeless than before. The weight he'd put on seemed to have found its way all round his body and even the cut of his suit couldn't hide it. He also had the shakes. A half empty bottle of whisky stood on the table, I could smell the morning's intake on his breath. Something had happened since I'd been away, something beyond his control.

'Prove it,' I challenged him.

'My generosity? In any way I can.'

'Buy the cafe.'

'From myself?'

'I'll sell you the title to it.'

'Barry's suicide note? How touching you'd consider selling it to me.'

'Ten grand.'

'You obviously cared a great deal for him to attach such a sum to a simple piece of paper.'

'Take it or leave it.'

'Oh, I'll leave it.'

It had been worth a try. I knew he'd never have bought the note, but at least it might have prompted him to put his hand in his pocket and dish out something for the two and a half years of my life he'd stolen from me. I reckoned I was well in credit even after deducting the bill for the penny arcade demolition job.

He stood up. I thought he was going to show me the door but he wrenched it open in a paranoid effort to catch someone peering through the keyhole. He ignored the startled look on the face of his secretary and slammed it shut again.

'You will choose not to believe this,' he started.

'Try me.'

'The cafe was mine. Barry was the manager. I installed him, he reported to me.'

'Yeah, well you would say that, wouldn't you.'

'Perhaps I would should I feel any need to justify myself to you – which I don't. I do, however, feel you deserve an explanation.'

'Good of you.'

'Consider for a moment why I tolerated you for so long. Employ your devious mind to the possibilities.'

'I'm not with you.'

'Let me make it easier. Why should I have taken such an interest in Barry's welfare? Why should I have let you go after the damage you caused?'

'Friendship.'

'Hardly. And finally, why don't you consider why Barry should have claimed the cafe to be his when all the time he knew it was mine?'

'According to you.'

'It's the truth.'

'I couldn't begin to guess.'

'Well, shall we just say that blood is thicker than water. My brother protected you more times than you could ever imagine.'

'Barry . . . your brother?'

'Yes. Now fuck off and don't pester me again or I'll have your bollocks for suspenders. And I mean it.'

# TWENTY-FOUR

SITTING ALONE OUTSIDE a pub, I tried to take in what Hollister had just told me. To this day, I've never been able to fathom why Barry and he wanted to keep their relationship secret. I suppose the answer lay somewhere in the complex web that held them together when they faced the combined assault of their upbringing in the respectable suburbs.

I didn't have time to dwell on it, the time had come to leave Brighton for good. It was a real wrench – leaving somewhere that had meant so much to me. There's something haughty and feminine about the town. It's unforgivably ugly and new in too many places but there's still enough life in the lofty old harlot for her to throw her skirts round you and haul you close for a long slow dance. People who come for the day never see that. The place is a bitch to the day tripper, they're coralled down the worst dog-shit-laden streets, the poorest fattiest restaurants, the most expensive pubs with the dirtiest glasses. But it serves them right. Stay away from my town.

I waited until the heat had gone out of the day, then walked west through the crowds on the prom towards Shoreham. To get a decent lift I knew I'd have been better off further inland but I reckoned I wouldn't get far before night set in. I had a rucksack with me which I'd taken as an afterthought from the cafe and, stuffed in the metal frame underneath, was a sleeping bag, so I knew I'd be alright if I had to kip outside for the night. I jacked a thumb at the stream of evening traffic, fixed a picture of May in my mind for luck and hoped someone was bored enough to be looking for some conversation on a long drive west.

After half an hour a lorry pulled up and a thick forearm jutted from the window of the high cab, followed by a meaty face. 'Where you going?'

'West.'

'Yeah. Where?'

'Dorset.'

The driver shouldered the door open and I climbed up the two metal steps into the cosy cab. The driver let off the air brakes and after a cursory glance in the mirror powered the long articulated lorry into the traffic. My attempts at making conversation were stonewalled; the driver just seemed to need the company, so I shut up and reviewed the last twenty-four hours of freedom. A peculiar calm had settled on me to join the residue of the glow from the booze and the last of the day's warmth rising from the tarmac to the cab. The sun dropped to dusk then disappeared altogether. A few miles later we pulled into a broad lorry park behind an all-night transport cafe. I declined the offer of a fry-up and curled up in the cab while the driver went off for his break. I was asleep when he came back and woke an hour or so later hearing him humming to the soft sounds of a late-night local radio station. It was nearly eleven, Brighton was already way behind. I made one final decision. I decided to give myself a week and if I hadn't found May by then I'd accept it as fate and move on.

The sleep had loaded me with optimism; the driver looked solid and in control. We were safe together crunching through the tarmac miles. Cars sped towards us out of the darkness chasing cones of light, each a time-capsule of hopes buried deep, each one like me heading towards something momentous. There is always something momentous ahead. There has to be. Maybe I got a taste of it in the prison cell. Maybe that's the big finish we're all lurching towards in our ignorance. But nobody really knows or the surprise would be ruined for the rest of us. And if we lost our ignorance then there'd be no more questions, nothing more worth saying. We'd all just sit around in the warm expectation of what we knew was in store for us. That's why we're not party to the information – somebody understands us well enough to withhold it.

I don't know, it seemed to make some sort of sense then: a minor revelation at the end of a long day of revelations.

'A'right mate?' the driver said, seeing that I'd woken.

And I was. For the first time in as long as I could remember I really was fine.

It didn't take long to locate the village that May had last written from. It was just a couple of miles inland from the Dorset coast, the house a mile or two to the west. The village seemed to have been settled by a gaggle of retired home counties bank manager types. You could spot the few remaining cottages owned by the legitimate locals; they were the ones with the cracked façades and numbers instead of clever nameplates. My rucksack drew a few scowls as I trudged past the 'Village Shoppe' and along the main street. I walked into the public bar of The Bull. The landlord was surly but loosened up when I checked out the availability of B&B. I laid some stuff on him about walking from Dover to Land's End for cancer. Charity always strikes a chord with people in the service sector – they can sniff the free advertising a mile off. I bought a pint of lukewarm beer, took a seat by the unlit fire and watched the locals trudge in across the flagstoned floor, throw a couple of stiffeners down and trudge out again cursing their ulcers.

Lunchtime came and the place filled out. A relay of sales reps arrived to feed their paunches with chips and beer which they consumed sullenly at invoice-laden tables. A man about my age in a sharp suit, a loud blue tie and a seventies glam rock haircut asked if he could take the chair opposite me. I was glad of the company.

'Camping?' he said in an agricultural accent after three quarters of his pint had worked its way into his bloodstream.

'No. Walking.'

'Yes? I used to walk.'

'For cancer.'

'Charity?'

'Yeah.'

'Good for you.' His mind was somewhere else. His eyes kept darting to the door.

'You waiting for somebody?'

'What?' He was immediately on the defensive.

'You look like you're waiting for somebody.'

'Do I? No I'm not. Old habit. Irritating habit. Sorry, I didn't mean to be rude. I was listening.'

'In that case,' I said, 'actually I'm not.'

'Not what?'

'Walking. I just made it up for the stiff behind the bar.'

'Geoff.'

'You know him?'

'No. It's purely a business relationship. Get you another?' He took my glass to 'Geoff' and returned with two packets of pork scratchings. 'So . . . ' He set the glasses carefully on the table. 'You're not camping and you're not walking for charity. Cheers.'

'Cheers. No . . . I've been in prison.'

'Prison, eh?' That one titillated him. That one dragged his eyes off the door and back to the action round the table. He appraised me, looking closely for signs of incarceration as I sketched in the details of the last couple of years. It was easy to tell it to a stranger, almost easier than turning it around in my own mind. He chipped in a few questions for clarification but didn't offer any judgement or advice. I liked him for that. I felt myself warming to him. He wasn't a professional pub type – not a real barfly with a ruddy complexion and a sardonic quip for every occasion. He seemed displaced, confused, drinking hard but without much relish, waiting for the liquid to kick in and lift him from his despair. He was trapped on the ledge of his youth, unsure whether to throw it all in and jump into the rising tide of middle age. 'You don't feel hard done by, then?' he said.

'I don't think so. It's all over. I feel as though I've left it behind, like it was somebody else.'

'That's good. Isn't it?'

'Yeah. I've not thought much about it.'

'Course you have.'

'Well, maybe.'

'Can't stop yourself. Same with me. Running things backwards and forwards, every which way. What's the point?'

'Go on then.'

'What?'

'Tell me about it,' I prompted. 'Your turn.'

'Me? I work for the council.'

'Doing what?'

'Well . . . I go round the county looking for piles of unlicensed waste, find out who put them there and prosecute the buggers. Keeps me off the streets.' He laughed to signal the joke, he'd told it before; it probably wasn't funny the first time round. But an idea was beginning to form in my mind and of course it involved exploiting Ray (his name dropped into the middle of the conversation with a formal handshake). I decided he could be my passport into Kit's Kosmic Castle where May was being held against her will. (This, of course, was by then the way I'd chosen to see it.) I egged Ray on and wished I hadn't. He started on a tirade against his ex-wife who'd gone off with a company director (she was his PA). This was where his bitterness lay, and some of it had been translated into blame which he was using effectively against himself. After all, if he'd been a better man she wouldn't have gone. I suspected the self pity was probably there before the woman left him and might have contributed to her departure but I decided not to forward it as a suggestion.

And so it went on. Ray had cornered me with the oldest trick in the book – feigned interest. All I could do was to switch off and force myself to keep my balance in relation to the four corners of the room. The beer had more of a kick to it than I'd first thought. Then May walked in.

'May,' I said blankly, like a stooge, like someone who'd seen a ghost. But it wasn't loud enough for her to hear as she walked up to the bar.

'Eh?' Ray broke his rhythm.

'May.'

'Blimey!' He craned his neck round for a better look. He had a boil on the back of his neck. She'd reached the bar, I heard her ask for change for the telephone.

'Introduce us.' He was drunk now.

'Shut up.'

'What?'

'Ray. Shut the fuck up.' That did it. I needed to concentrate. I'd booked myself into the pub for a reason: I needed the time alone to decide how I was going to make my approach. I didn't want her rejecting me on the strength of some stupid blunder I might make when we first met.

The hardest thing was not knowing who it was I was going to meet. The May at the bar was not the May I had known – that much was immediately clear. She looked self-assured; in control. Her hair had been tinted blonde and cut boyishly short, she'd filled out round her bum and her Levis accentuated her lush curves. She was rounder, more whole, more wholesome. And her poise struck a real stance: right hand dug deep into her back pocket, left hand tapping with controlled and telling impatience on the counter. The man next to her tried to hit on her. She said something, he laughed and turned to his mate tilting his glass in her direction. 'She's alright,' his gesture was saying. 'She's alright.'

Ray looked wounded. I didn't want him blurting anything else out and drawing her attention to us so I apologised while trying to keep my eyes on what she was up to.

'No chance,' Ray said slyly from the corner of his mouth.

'Mm?' Geoff was making a meal of handing over her change, lingering too long as he dropped the money into her palm.

'You and her. No way.'

'For Christ's sake.' She was walking out now, a dozen pairs of eyes turned in her direction as she opened the door. As it swung shut behind her the tension in the room diminished.

'May. Over here!' Ray called and then guffawed. But she was already gone.

'Idiot.'

'I thought you wanted to talk to her.'

'Look, just keep your nose out of it.'

'I just thought . . . '

'Well don't.'

'Fine.' He brooded over his half inch of beer, sipping it thoughtfully. I wanted some time on my own, but the thought of using Ray as a Trojan Horse was becoming more attractive.

'My shout,' I said brightly. I'd made a decision. I was going to go to her. I didn't want to run the risk of her coming to me.

'You're bloody unhinged, you are,' he said as I delivered the third pint of poison.

'Am I?'

'A girl like that and a jailbird like you. No way, José.'

'You don't know her and you don't know me so shut it.'

'Oh I know you – you think I wasn't listening? – I was. You just haven't got a bloody clue, have you.'

This was deeply unsettling. Either Ray had drunk himself sober, or something I'd said or done had jolted him back to earth. Perhaps I was going in too hard on him. The etiquette on the wing is to go in hard and fast and never mind the consequences; I'd forgotten it was different in the real world. But May . . . May was a dream. She looked as though she'd been earthed, tethered back to the ground and sewn back together with invisible thread.

Ray lurched to his feet. 'I'm going for a piss. Look after my briefcase.' When he stumbled back doing up his fly he seemed to have been gone for no more than ten seconds. He'd pissed on his turn-up. He sat and exhaled with the effort of the journey.

'I want you to do something for me,' I said.

'Oh, best mates now, are we? Think I owe you one or something?'

'No. Nothing like that. I'll ask you and if you don't want to do it, then don't.'

'Don't worry about that.'

'Tomorrow morning . . . '

'Working.' He belched the word onto the back of his hand.

'Tomorrow morning drive me out to May's place. Pretend you're on official business and I'm working with you.'

'What for?'

'So I don't have to explain to some hippy what I'm doing there. I just want you to get me in. That's all.'

'Why should I?'

'You tell me.'

'Why not? See you making a fool of yourself in front of wonder woman. Might be a laugh?'

'You're a mate.'

'I thought I was a sad case but you really take the biscuit, don't you.'

At closing time I went upstairs to my room. The smell of the public bar wafted up through the floor and cloaked the bedding and utilitarian furniture in a layer of fine dust and cigarette smoke. For a while I watched the street through the small netted window. Geoff was chivvying the lunchtime stragglers out by waving a tea towel at them. A few cars passed but there was no more activity, the aged populace seemed to be taking a siesta.

By then I was no longer afraid that I wouldn't catch up with May again. Even just seeing her had re-cemented a bond between us; if she'd seen me I was pretty sure that she'd have felt the same. It was all becoming clear. Of course she still wanted me – we were born to be together. The times we spent in Brighton, the mad afternoons shoplifting, the night on the pier . . . how could there not be a future for us after we'd shared all that? And the night in the show house watching the sun going down. That was the real beginning of it for us, being inside, being close, sowing the seed for our future. I was crazy to react the way I did when she wrote and said she was starting to work out things for herself. What use was she to me in that state? What use was she to herself? But now she had worked it through and we were ready to meet again.

I stayed out of the bar that night and instead took a long walk to the sea. When I came back I had a shower and laid out my clothes for the next day like a groom on the night before his wedding. I wanted to do it right. I wanted to take flowers and run towards her across a wide expanse of green then swing her round so her legs were flying like you see on the telly. I went to bed full of hope and fell straight asleep.

When I awoke the next morning to the sound of a tractor passing I was aware of having had only one dream – the dream of the thin brown room, strangely absent from my time in prison. Only this time it was different. The woman was no longer protesting at the intrusion of the brutal visitor. 'Now,' she said as he forced her onto the bed. 'Now.'

# TWENTY-FIVE

I WENT DOWN for breakfast and found the dining room behind the public bar. Geoff was acting as waiter in a fresh cardigan. There was no sign that he'd been up until past midnight cleaning glasses and polishing the bar.

'Sleep well?'

'Fine. Thanks.'

'Full English breakfast?'

Before I could say anything he was off through the swing door and fetching it. I felt rough. The previous day's session with Ray had unsettled me and all the things I thought I'd sorted out in my head now seemed to make no sense at all. My motives were all over the place; analysing them further I realised they'd been pretty skewed even before I got May's last letter.

The breakfast was fiercely hot and fatty. I pushed it away and concentrated on the coffee. I felt very much alone. I remembered feeling pretty much the same shortly after I'd joined the army. Up until that point I'd always used my solitary status to my advantage. As a kid it was always assumed by grown ups that I was with my parents, in truth I was often alone but diverted attention from myself with fluent lies. When I was nine I ran away from the home and spent a week in Skegness. I fell in with a family who shared their lunch with me each day on the beach. At night I slept in a small park. I never minded the solitude. The home gave me all the stability I wanted, there was always a matron around for those moments when a mother's attention was absolutely necessary. I left at sixteen, already prepared for the adult world, and had no problem making my way from place to place supported by the proceeds of petty theft and various short-term jobs. There was a moment in my life when I could have graduated into more serious crime. I was just at the edge of a circle of petty villains who were planning a series of raids on sub post offices. They were intending to hit five in as many days, criss-crossing the capital so the robbery squad wouldn't know how to deploy their resources. At that point I got out of it and joined the army.

The recruiting officer wanted to put me down for officer training. He said I had the type of intelligence the army valued. But I wanted the anonymity of the ranks. So I joined and, as I said, soon felt the unfamiliar despair of loneliness. There was more implied concern from even the smallest gesture of friendship from a previously bawling Drill Sergeant than in any amount of affection handed out at the home. And that's what got me every time. They couldn't understand it: I'd face any bollocking they handed out – but if somebody asked how I was I'd be reduced to tears. They sent me to the shrink but he was too caught up in pat theories to say anything that made any sense. So that was that.

Now it seems like it all happened to somebody else and my history was much more mundane. The truth is that it wasn't. One day I'll write it all down (all the stuff about London, the bit about the year I spent with the lecturer and his wife, the sad time under the needle, the six months in Paris – all of that) and the chapter on Barry and May will shrink back down to size. But since I'd met May, nothing else really mattered. Everything that happened before seemed to be just an overture to her, everything since a prelude to our meeting again. Except the closer that meeting came the harder I was forced to examine the possibility that maybe it wouldn't work out. And what then? What then?

The prospect of starting all over again with another Barry in another town for another two or three years was just too dreadful to contemplate. Even the thought of going back to Mary and becoming an Arthur to her was a more attractive option.

'. . . Take this?' Geoff had skated back, hurrying it along.

'Thanks.'

'Can we expect you tonight?'

'Yes. I'll stay one more night.'

'Lovely. More coffee?'

'Please.' I'd earned a re-fill. If I'd chosen not to stay I knew the offer wouldn't have been made.

'Ah – your friend,' he said, returning with the coffee.

'Friend?'

'In the bar yesterday.'

'Oh, Ray. No, he's not a friend – I mean I just met him then.'

'I shall have to bar him.'

'Well you'll have to tell him, not me.'

'Just so long as you know.'

He avoided my eyes and walked out. I knew I should have said something to him, at least offered a token defence for Ray. I could have struck back by complaining about the food but what was the point? I was never good at complaining. Barry was the same. If he'd been there we'd both have got pissed off about the quality of the breakfast. Then we'd have ended up arguing because neither of us liked to admit we were being ripped off. Then we'd feel bad about it and spend the rest of the day cocooned from the rest of the world feeling sorry for ourselves and glad that at least we had each other. But of course Barry wasn't there, even though I had a strong feeling that he was watching over me. Geoff annoyed me even more by carrying a copy of the *Daily Mail* under his arm like a swagger stick as he stalked off for his daily moment of peace on the bog.

I toyed with the idea of trying to get into the till but decided it wasn't worth the risk. Instead I went back up to my room and walked in on a cleaner rummaging through my rucksack. I stood there watching her. She hadn't heard me come in.

'See anything you like?'

'Oh God.' She jumped but didn't turn round and fumbled for a cigarette from her apron, her back still turned. She had long thin hair and wore a faded pale blue cotton dress, sweat had formed two half moons beneath her arms. The cigarette wouldn't light. She was getting more and more angry with herself, her movements becoming more fractious.

'Never mind,' I said. 'It doesn't matter.'

'I knew you'd say that.'

'What?' The hair stood up on my neck. I sensed danger.

'I knew.'

'How. How did you know?'

'I knew you'd be good to me.'

'Turn round.' I wanted to go closer to her but the space around her was charged and full. I couldn't penetrate it.

'No.'

'I said turn round.'

'You come here.'

I went in cautiously. I remembered seeing a film like this. A man chased a dwarf in a red hooded coat. He finally caught up with it. It turned and stabbed him to death.

'Come on. Come here. I've got something of yours.' The voice was calmer now but still brittle. I closed the door and walked in. Then I heard a hammering – loud and penetrating. 'Closer . . . come closer.' The figure swung round as I approached her. The first thing I saw was the glint of something in her hand. I knew what it was immediately: it was the hook, Barry's hook, the hook from the roof of his living room. The second thing I registered in that long split second as the hammering persisted outside was her face. It was May. The old May. Angry and insane and ready to wreak havoc with the sharp metal.

I'd read about dreams like that. Dreams of awakening. They can go on for ever, each horror followed by a further awakening. But one was enough for me. The sheets were twisted and damp. The hammering had become Geoff banging the door and shouting, 'Breakfast.' I shouted back and he went away. I showered and re-ran the dream. I was surprised at how easily I'd acknowledged the possibility that May wouldn't want to pick up the threads of our relationship. I ached for company and banal conversation so I went downstairs for breakfast and found the dining room exactly where I'd dreamt it. But Geoff wasn't serving and there were others in the room. The food was better and the coffee stronger. I eagerly embarked on a conversation about the weather with a tie-less, besuited sales rep poring over the *Mail* on the next table. He threw in a bit about driving conditions and the long-range forecast and I went back up feeling completely re-charged and more optimistic about the day.

I combed my hair and shaved with a new blade. The water was as hot as I could bear and the soap lathered easily. But I didn't much like the look I encountered in my eyes when I faced them in the mirror: it was veiled, suspicious. My skin still carried the lacklustre, almost transparent institutional hue which needed grilling off with a few days on the beach. A few flecks of grey had appeared in my hair which was now down to my shoulders. Gravity was making my mouth droop like a Zapata moustache. All in all it could have been more appealing and I felt even worse when Ray turned up and handed me a clipboard and torch. He claimed I'd need the props for authenticity but I refused them so he made me wear a peaked hat instead. When I put it on, he exploded with a nasal laugh, determined to turn the whole episode into a huge joke.

So we drove off and I faced the prospect of the most important meeting of my life dressed like some celestial meter reader.

# TWENTY-SIX

WE APPROACHED THE house down a long drive which spilled out into the expanse of the garden. The place looked as though it ad been a Victorian country retreat – large, fading white – that now eeded money spending on it. We parked and walked across the ravel then through a pair of ivied pillars that supported the canopied ntrance. Large picture windows on each side of the main door oked out onto a set of overgrown lawns that petered away into a rid of hedged fields. The sea was visible as a distant silver glint.

The impressive location had sobered Ray's attitude and curtailed e stream of irritating banter he'd been venting on the journey. Ie'd spent too much time living alone; I suspected him to be the pe of person who'd be just as happy to talk to himself as anyone se. I pressed the bell but nobody came to the door so we walked nto the entrance hall. The marble floor was a mess of bicycles and vellington boots, discarded raincoats and cardboard boxes. A voman was rummaging through a tea chest. Her long lank hair was rey with a rumour of blonde, she wore odd-coloured socks, her lothes were an ill conceived mix of cheesecloth and knitted atchwork squares. It looked as though she'd missed the magic bus om the sixties and had to walk all the way.

'I'm looking for the other one of these.' She held up a mud-ncrusted walking boot. 'I shall have to borrow one. I don't suppose hey'll mind, will they?' She looked to us for reassurance.

'Kit might,' I floated.

'Oh well, he'll just have to go on minding, won't he? Have yo
seen my scarf?'

'The red one?' Ray improvised.

'Blue.'

'I think May borrowed it,' I said.

'Well she could have asked.'

'We could get it back if you like,' Ray said.

'No, thank you.'

Ray had blown it by adopting a sinister look and jotting somethin
down on his clipboard.

'What do you want?'

'We're friends. Friends of May,' he said.

'You look like a policeman.'

'Accountant,' said Ray unconvincingly. 'We're accountants.'

The woman peered at us more closely. 'Anyway, I have to get int
town.' She seemed to have dismissed the threat. 'I think she mus
have my bicycle.' She wandered off through a large double door a
the bottom of the wide staircase and into a room where somebod
was playing a piano. We followed her through.

'That's lovely,' she said to the young, swaying woman at th
keyboard.

'It's Chopin.'

'Lovely. Have you seen my bike?'

'I think they were cleaning it. In the kitchen. The children wer
looking for a bike to clean.'

'The kitchen?' She disappeared through a pair of open Frenc
windows and turned left and out of sight.

'We'll wait here,' Ray called after she was clearly out of earsho
He sat on a sofa and loosened his coat. 'My sister plays the piano,' h
volunteered.

'And do you?' The woman continued playing, swaying back an
forth as she poured her heart into the music.

'No . . . I'm a banjo man myself.' He jumped up, stifling a laugh
and went to the bookcase where he drew out a thick volume
'Gibbon,' he said, carrying it two-handed back to the sofa. 'I find h
bears re-reading, doesn't he?' I left him flicking through the boo

ıd followed in the path of the scarfless woman. The music stopped
ıd I heard a conversation begin. I knew I'd been right in taking him
ong even if it hadn't quite worked out how we'd planned.

The house jutted out at the back with a single added-on storey
hich was newer than the rest but in equal need of repair. There was
nough of the garden left to indicate where the flower beds had been
ut not enough for them to be reclaimable. A small boy darted from a
ıicket of dry grass much taller than he was; he was followed Indian
le by an older girl then two other boys. Further down the garden a
lume of fragrant woodsmoke rose vertically from a bonfire. A long
ne of static washing was strung from the back wall to the lowest
ranch of a tree. A tent was pitched close to the house. I heard
ughter from an upstairs room, then a bath started emptying into a
aky pipe, sending a shower of suds into a deckchair below. It wasn't
ow I'd imagined. I'd prepared myself for anarchy not domesticity.

I walked past the dim kitchen where the woman was reclaiming
er bike from a posse of protesting children. A man was working at
ıe stove, stirring something with his right hand and reading a book
ropped up on a music stand. Another man suddenly emerged from
ıe kitchen door. He was carrying a hammer and wearing combat
ıtigues. His hair had been hacked to a short bristle, he had a stud in
is nose and a goatee beard.

'Yes?' he challenged.

'I've come to see May.'

'Yes?'

'Yes.'

'You've not been here before.'

'So what?'

'Why do you want to see her?'

'That's between me and her.'

'Not if you don't change the heavy attitude, it isn't.'

'Is that right?'

'That is right.' He weighed the hammer against his palm.

'I'm sorry. I'm her brother.'

'Strike one!'

'Alright. I'm a friend. Just tell me where she is. I'm not here t
cause trouble.'

'You look like a troublemaker.'

'Let me see Kit, then.'

'You still haven't told me who you are. You could be the filth.'

'I'm not.'

'Army then. Secret Services.'

'Look. Take me to May, she'll vouch for me.'

'I want you to tell me.'

'I'm a friend. What more can I say?'

'Alright. You pass the audition.' He turned heel and stalked off
The scarfless woman wheeled her bike out of the kitchen.

'It's terribly wet. Will it rust, do you think?' She said with studie
vagueness.

'Not immediately.'

'Good. I have to go to town, you see.'

'Yes. You said.'

'Did you say you were looking for May?'

'No. But I am.'

'You should find her upstairs. I think they're taking class. Are the
taking class?' she called to the figure in the kitchen.

'Yes. They're in the blue room.'

'Thanks,' I said, but she didn't move off.

'I'm just a visitor here really.' She freewheeled her bicycl
forwards and backwards on the spot.

'I guessed that.'

'And it's been very good for me. Particularly Kit. Kit's bee
particularly understanding . . . considering . . . well, I had little trus
. . . in men.'

A small urchin child of indeterminate sex came through the door
'Have you finished with the bike?'

'No I haven't. And I'm talking.'

The child remained rooted to the spot.

'I'll bring it back when I've finished. Now run away.' The chil
went back in, trailing a glance at me and the bike. 'One of the polit
ones,' the woman said with regret, 'one of the lesser free spirits.

sometimes wonder how they'll turn out. But then I look at how we turned out and know there must be a better way.'

'A better way?'

'Oh, I couldn't begin . . . ask May. We work on all sorts of things: TA, Gestalt, Psychodrama, Primal Therapy. William is the Primal Therapist.' William, it seemed from her fond look towards the kitchen, was the cook. 'It's a case of discovering something that works for you. But that makes it sound rather formal. It's not formal. We work on consensus . . . and sharing. And openness.'

'Sounds healthy,' I said sceptically.

' . . . And those who come to mock tend to leave . . . well, much changed.'

'What are you trying to tell me?'

'If you came here looking for someone, you may find somebody quite different.' She put her right foot on the pedal and pushed off, mounting her bike as it picked up speed. Her scarf hung loosely, dangling dangerously close to the chain.

I went into the kitchen. The brown-tiled floor was puddled with water; an old galvanised tin bath stood by the range. The room was dark and smelt of bread. A long scrubbed pine table ran the full width. I counted fifteen assorted wooden chairs in varying degrees of disrepair placed at eccentric angles around it. The Primal Therapist kept his eyes fixed on the thick text as I walked past him. I reached the bottom of the back staircase and climbed towards the sound of children. Chanting gave way to laughter and screams, a man's voice cut in and the noise diminished. I bumped into Ray on the landing.

'I'm looking for the bog,' he said. 'I suppose they use one here – or do you reckon they recycle it all?'

'Evens bet I should think.'

'What have you found out?'

'Nothing. Not much anyway.'

'I have. From the pianist.' He was eager to impart the results of his foray. 'It's not a squat. It's a sort of sanctuary for loony alternatives: holistic photography, knit your own muesli, that sort of thing. The place is owned by your friend Kit. He's the man with the cash. If you fall out with him you're out. Otherwise you can hang around at his expense until you get your head together, man.'

The noise in the classroom died altogether. A story was being told.

'Look.' Ray was serious for the first time that day. 'She's in there.' He pointed towards the classroom. 'And she's got a kiddie with her.'

'Right,' I said, swallowing hard. 'Thanks.'

'... You won't do anything stupid, will you?'

'No.'

'Good luck then, mate.' He bear-hugged me. I was shaking and again thanked God I'd brought him with me. He went down the stairs and I walked on along the corridor, the pressure building in my chest. I reached the classroom and peered cagily in through the half-glass door. A group of kids sat cross-legged on the floor surrounding a Canute-like figure that was unmistakably Kit. Only it wasn't the Kit of my imagination. This one was older – fifty, maybe more. He was not bald nor did he sport earrings or a pony tail. He was dressed unspectacularly in thick bottle-green cord trousers and an open-necked khaki shirt. He was charismatic, grey-bearded and black-haired and possessed a voice that seemed to resonate through the whole fabric of the building. The tale he was telling was of far away and there seemed little doubt that this was where his distant gaze lay. But this Canute was not enthroned on a beach, he sat awkwardly in a wheelchair; his polio-twisted frame seemed small and wasted; his left arm was cradled dead in his lap; with his right he punctuated his story.

Then, looking in the direction of his gaze, I saw what he was staring at. It was May, sitting in a chair by the open window, luxuriating in the sun on her back. Her eyes were alive with a smile, her face open and composed and at her feet a girl; a small dirt-smudged blonde girl drawing finger pictures in the dust on the floor. The child was the spitting image of her: they were the first and last in a set of Russian dolls. I hesitated with my hand on the handle but I couldn't go in. There was something between her, the child and the king on his throne that excluded everyone else in the room, and seeing that link I knew there was nothing more to say; no point in going in; no point in asking whether she remembered me or why she hadn't written or visited. She and the child were the far-away place Kit was staring at and there was no room there for anybody else.

The story ended. The children scrambled to their feet and made mob-handed for the door. I stepped back into the shadows and they spilled past towards the back stairs. Then the classroom was empty bar Kit, May and the child. I waited and listened but their voices had dropped and all I could pick up on was the tone of the conversation: comfortable and domestic. All of my doubts surfaced at the same time, swamping my hope. The prison had taken a toll on me in a way I was only now understanding, sapping the strength I needed to operate in a world where people come and go whether you want them to or not. I didn't have the strength to go in.

I set off back towards the stairs: carefully, quietly. I didn't want to draw their attention to me, I just wanted to run to somewhere I could make sense of what I had seen. But then I heard the pad of feet in the corridor: a child loosed from its leash running towards me. Then the tiny version of May tore past; unsteady but determined.

'Be careful of the stairs!' At the sound of May's voice I froze as though the warning had been called to me. The child ran on, unheeding.

'Be careful,' I shouted. The child stopped dead. But the novelty of the voice stopped her only for a split second, then she sat on the top step and bumped away down the stairs on her backside. Footsteps were coming towards me from behind. I tensed. I wanted to run. I wanted to turn to face her in the way I had planned but I was powerless.

'You came then,' she said to my back. I felt her hand on my shoulder. The touch lacked tenderness as she pulled me round to face her. 'You look terrible.'

'Prison issue,' I said, wilfully misunderstanding her and opening the jacket to reveal the lack of a respectable label. But her angry eyes hadn't moved from my face.

'Is she what you expected. Our child?' She weighed whether to spring or withdraw.

'I can see you in her. I don't see anything of me.'

'They say you can't see yourself. It's true. But I see you in her all the time . . . It was painful. But not any more.'

I had a sense that May had worked out this speech long before.

'You seem . . . comfortable.' I stepped away, back along the corridor. I couldn't keep the bitterness from my voice.

'I've made my own comfort, Cliffie. I had to. I had nobody to make it for me.' There was a hardness in her that hadn't been there before.

Kit emerged in his wheelchair from the classroom. It was clear he'd been listening. 'Stay with us for a while,' he offered in the cultured voice of reason.

'I've just come out of prison. I'm not going to swap one set of walls for another.'

'Anger is good.' Kit laid his hand on my arm like a healer. 'It is good.' I backed further away from the shock of the contact.

'I wrote,' I said. 'I wrote twice . . . I did all I could to get in touch. I didn't leave you by choice. You were all I had.'

May stared for a while then whispered something in Kit's ear. He went back into the classroom and gently closed the door behind him.

'Let's go outside.' May took my hand and I allowed her to lead me down the stairs and out into the garden. We walked past the overgrown flower beds and through a small orchard of trees. Finally we came to a wooden bench far from the oppressive house and May guided me down beside her.

We talked for an hour. Or, mostly, she talked. And when she did it was of her life before we'd met. Of her first child and her father and mother, even of what she remembered of Edie and Ron. She told her story as if it was leading to something: to some moral which would illuminate what was going to happen to us. But when she finished she prompted me to do the same and I went back to events I had not thought of for years.

And when I left I felt easier in my mind. It had been good to see her but she held none of the answers I needed. The only thing left between us was the child. But the child was May's. Not mine. She had found her own way and she made it clear that whether I had contacted her or not was almost irrelevant. I could not have been there at time she needed me most. But it was in those three years, as she waited for me, that she found herself.

I hitched a lift to London and arrived glad to embrace the anonymity of the City. I rented a room in Earl's Court and made tentative moves back into the world – each day staying out longer, some nights not returning at all. After a week I found a job behind the bar of a club. The long hours suited me, the small impersonal room was a bonus and the manager proved to be decent enough when his wife had made up her mind that she could trust me. And when I knew I was going to stay for a while I wrote to May and sent her my address. She wrote back and we established a contact that has survived unbroken to this day.

It was in writing to her that I began to understand what she was beginning to tell me in the garden. Because she encouraged me to tell her about my past, not my present. And her letters back to me never failed to acknowledge something she had found of value in what I told her. It would be too easy to believe that the good she salvaged from my memories had any bearing on the value I began to place in them – I was too aware of having played that role with Barry. Being forced to go back through it all, I discovered moments which came up sharp and clean when I burnished them. But our correspondence stopped short of the cafe and my life with Barry and with her. Perhaps it was in my friendship with the old bloke that I learned how important these memories are. And there are good memories – somewhere in there. But they remain in the only drawer I can lock in my room and the fact that you are reading them now means that I have chosen to trust you. Unless you have stolen them from me.

I have May's latest letter in front of me. The child; her child: Hope (not a name I would have chosen but not as extreme as I had feared) will be fourteen years old next month and May wonders in her usual casual way whether I wouldn't like to go to her party. It's an offer she's made each year and each year I've refused. This time she's enclosed a note from Hope; a dignified teenage, take-it-or-leave-it account of her friends and her life. It's addressed to 'my distant father'. Enough time has passed for us now to have realistic expectations of each other. Perhaps, at last, it's time for us to meet.